The Case of the Curse of Houl

Rhiannon D. Elton

The Case of the Curse of Houl © Rhiannon D. Elton 2020
The Wolflock Cases: Book 3

First Edition July 2019
Second Edition March 2020

ISBN: 978-0-6487636-3-5 (paperback)

info@rhiannoneltonauthor.com

Cover compiled by Rhiannon D. Elton

Cataloguing-in-Publication information for this title is listed with the National Library of Australia.

Published in Australia by Rhiannon D. Elton and Pelaia Adventures

*Dedicated to Mum and Grandma
for putting the fear of death into me about
eating undercooked food.*

Get More of the Magic & Mystery…

subscribe.rhiannoneltonauthor.com/more

If you want more clues, more magic and more mystery, let me know by going to the Case of the Cure of Houl subscribe page.

You'll get clues, maps, sketches, behind the scenes stories, lore and much more! You'll also be the first to know when a new story is coming out so you can solve the mystery before your friends.

If you sign up with the magical link below, you'll also get a free downloadable map to follow Wolflock's journey to Mystentine University.

subscribe.rhiannoneltonauthor.com/more

Declaration of Intention

Merry meet,

The purpose of the books the author writes is to give representation to as many peoples, creatures and landscapes as they can. Although written from the perspective of a Caucasian teenage boy, the author hopes to offer a light into the harmony of different cultures and creeds of people. The author's aim is to promote harmony, understanding and compassion in all areas, while also inspiring readers to stand up against injustice and be critical thinkers in life.

While the author does their best to research, interview and highlight the best parts of people, they are only human and can make mistakes. The author asks you gently educate them by sending them an email in order to discuss anything that may have caused harm to a group of people unintentionally.

The author believes that the cure for ignorance is education, but please approach the topic cordially in order to avoid any knee-jerk cognitive dissonance.

Finally, the viewpoints displayed in the books comes from a particular character and is not necessarily that of the author's. The author seeks to display flaws, growth and human nature on many levels, and hopes that you will analyse the character of the protagonist without adopting any negative behaviours from them.

Merry part, and merry meet again.

Rhiannon D'Elton

CHAPTER 1

Merry Part

It was a misty morning as the fresh chill of impending dawn lit the soft grey sky over the broad Zilber River. The muted orange leaves didn't even twitch, holding onto their glittering dewdrops like frozen gemstones. They were only woken when the breeze rose with the sun. No creature, fish or bird moved an inch in this lifelike painting of North Grothener.

The only movement came from the Silver Ice Hair as it streamed up the river. The comforting morning silence was disturbed only by the gentle splitting of the water by the mighty grey vessel as it cut through the river like scissors gliding through satin. Wolflock slept soundly, his ink stained hand drooping out from his bunk and into the kiss of the chilly morning air. It had been three days since he had been tricked into working for the captain, but, as the work itself was merely writing letters for the crew, he didn't protest beyond being a bit too familiar and sarcastic with Captain Blutro.

Wolflock suspected the captain knew he possessed significant linguistic skills, which allowed him to be safe from any hard labour. The crew were excited to utilise his skills when he told them he knew how to speak, read, and write in five languages. He was fluent in his native tongue of North Grothien, also known as Nördlicherwald, South Grothien language Plain e'sud, Dwyrrain from East Grothien, Corlesian merchant's tongue, and Puinteylien, the common language that everyone was taught. The crew were particularly excited as many of them could not read or write in foreign languages, only speak them. This gave them the chance to communicate with many of the friends they'd made over the years.

Wolflock had, so far, written for Grogen, who had twenty letters to write to all kinds of friends he'd made. Grogen said he tried to send them on a quarterly basis and didn't mind at all that so few people wrote back.

"It's hard to catch a moving ship," he'd chuckled as Wolflock scribbled away for him.

Hognut had only wanted to send a simple small note to the man who made his pipe, telling him it was still in good shape and that he wouldn't need another yet.

He wrote for Goden, who told his brother of daring battles with giant fish and the savage maramuti attack.

Geagle had asked him to send letters to two ladies telling them he had fallen in love and could no longer pursue them, but he still wished them the utmost happiness, adding that should they ever need transport up and down the river he'd be there to aid them. He had to write Geagle's letters three times because he couldn't decide on the right saccharine words to pour over his past beloveds to 'ease their pain of losing him'.

Wolflock also wrote for himself to Myna again, since he was not yet able to send the letters and she was unable to reply, she couldn't give him an indication on whether he should write to his father as well.

Not wanting any of the company to know he had been fooled into indentured employment, he let them think he was doing this from the kindness of his heart. Ever since he apologised to those he'd offended; the crew and company had been rather friendly toward him. His current 'charitable' acts only heightened the fondness they displayed. Wolflock had informed Mothy the day before that acts of altruism often brought this degree of fondness and that it could be used to their advantage, to which Mothy had laughed at him.

But what Wolflock had said held substance. The crew and passengers had permitted all kinds of mischief to take place and Wolflock was thrilled. Without many books to read and only a limited number of games to play, the passengers grew easily bored, which made Wolflock and Mothy's mischievous antics all the more entertaining.

Every night they snuck out to go and watch the stars from the crow's nest and tell stories about their lives. No one ever stopped them on their nightly venture, but they took delight in waking them in the early hours. The boys had also taken a set of drying white sheets and ran around the deck pretending to be ghosts. They had run around, trying to startle the other passengers until they crashed into each other. Captain Blutro and Slavidus had lectured them on how it was bad form to talk about the dead on a ship, especially for fun.

They tried to teach a maramuti to steal people's underwear from the drying line and then put them on, but they could only manage the first part. Ever since they saw the brigade of fairies migrating South, the maramuti had been regular residents on the ship. The cheeky, monkey-like creatures often used the rigging as a jungle gym or shocked passengers by ogling them through the windows first thing in the morning with their bulging eyes and pug faces. They seemed to enjoy listening to music and trying to dance along with the passengers, often slapping their broad flat tails on the deck or railing. Groger had been so shocked to see a maramuti racing about the deck with a pair of his floral shorts flapping about for everyone to see that the captain issued a ship-wide lockdown on all loose possessions. All doors were to be shut and locked and all crates to be fastened to discourage any playful theft.

Another time, Wolflock and Mothy had taken two planks of wood, tied them to their feet and 'skied' behind the ship until they lost the planks. Wolflock protested it had been a fish that caused him to get soaked and lose the wood, so, naturally, the boys made a huge show of looking for the wood stealing monster fish to try to stay out of trouble. It didn't work.

They had also tied themselves to one of the crossbeams on the sails and "flew" around the ship. When they realised that no one could reach them and that the crew were too busy to get them down they started shouting obscenities to the raucous laughter of the passengers passing by. It wasn't the shouting of "Grogen's running sky-clad on the deck again!" or "Froderyk's flipper feet!" that got them in trouble. It was when they swung too hard at the same time and the sails turned, steering the ship towards the bank for a good frightening minute. The crew scrambled to attention, and both boys were removed from the sail and given a stern talking to.

They had been made to swab the whole deck for the rest of the day and peel vegetables for dinner. Although he bemoaned his fate, Wolflock entertained himself by turning the mopping into a synchronised dance with Mothy, mirroring his movements from across the ship and freezing whenever anyone looked their way. When he got near enough Wolflock splashed him with the wet mop and they chased each other around the deck, slipping and sliding on the fresh wood as they brandished their mops like swords.

While peeling potatoes, turnips and beets, Wolflock and Mothy shared their stories with the crew and passengers about the animals they saw on the banks that day. Deer, maramuti, squirrels and birds, even a bear. Both of them swore they even saw a great stone creature wander off into the forest just beyond the tree line.

They never seemed to run out of topics to talk about.

The maramuti had also become regular inhabitants on the ship, dropping tuiti fruit and trying to 'exchange' it for other items. The sweet, vibrant green and pink tuiti fruit had become a staple part of their diet. Uhnha had taught Grogen, Mothy and Wolflock how to prepare the fruit in a variety of different ways, but the flavours became too strong and persistent for Wolflock's tastes. He had grown up with enough variety in food to be a picky eater and did not share the same propensity for sweet foods as his sister or Mothy.

The memories of the past few days danced through his dreams as Wolflock slept soundly in his cabin. It wasn't until an icy breeze cut across his face that he woke with a frown. Blinking slowly awake he sat up and looked at his porthole window. One of the maramuti, with its great big brown eyes and flat squashed face, was watching him carefully as it laid its hand by his hair comb.

"Shoo," he groaned and waved the creature away. "You can't have my comb. Now, be off with you."

He tried to reach for the window to latch it, but, as he did, he heard voices from directly above his room.

"Are you sure you won't stay until breakfast?"

Captain Blutro asked with a gentle tone. "I'm sure everyone would like to see you off,"

"We cannot," Ungul responded, her deep voice melodic and resigned. "If we do not leave at Ibhuloho Yomthi, we will miss our transport back home. Thank you for the offer."

"Please let Mothy know we wanted to say a proper goodbye, but I could not bear to see him cry," Uhnha sniffled.

"Aye. I'll let him know."

Wolflock's gut dropped.

"Wait!" he shouted and poked his head out of the window.

The noise brought them all over to the railing, looking down on him in surprise.

"Don't go! I'll be right up!"

He threw his monogrammed dressing gown and matching slippers on and flung himself into Mothy's room. His friend was in one of his usual sleeping positions, belly down, with one hand up the wall and one leg trying to reach the wall on the opposite side of the room. Wolflock flicked his ear and the blond boy went into spider-like convulsions, arms and legs twitching and flailing about spastically.

"Wha' cha do tha' for?" he grumbled and rubbed

his eyes, picking himself off the floor.

"You know, I never get tired of seeing you wake up. The process is fascinating and invigorating at the same time."

"Glad you feel energized," Mothy yawned and tried to crawl back into bed.

"Oi! No, you don't! The Blickland sisters are leaving soon and they want to see you before they go," he said as he grabbed Mothy's foot.

"What?" Mothy blinked as his mind slowly began engaging. "I have to give them something. They haven't left yet, have they?"

"Not yet, but we don't have long." Wolflock yanked him by the arm into the hall.

Mothy grabbed his bag, adding even more weight Wolflock had to drag up the stairs. They emerged in the brisk morning, the fresh tinge of pine needles in the air.

"I must insist you let me at least stop for just an hour," Captain Blutro protested.

"We will not be responsible for everyone else being late to their destination." Ungul frowned and folded her arms defiantly. "Our agreement was that we would leave without you stopping; I will not incur a debt because we surrendered to sentiment-"

"Unhna! Ungul!" Mothy called out. "I have

something for you."

"Oh Mothy," Unhna sighed and hugged him tightly. "I'm so glad we got to see you before we left."

Captain Blutro and Ungul stood with their mouths open at the boys' sudden appearance.

"How did you wake him?" Ungul's face broke into an amazed smile.

Wolflock puffed his chest out proudly. "I have my ways."

"He flicked your ear?" Uhnha rolled her eyes to Mothy.

"He flicked my ear."

The ladies chuckled as Wolflock deflated.

"These are for both of you. Please keep them safe. They're meant to keep our hearts connected so that if we are ever near each other's path again, we can wish one another a merry meet." Mothy said as he held out two small, wooden rabbits with a glittering white and pink opal in their chests.

"Mothy... This is beautiful. Thank you," Ungul breathed.

"Oh, you precious, precious boy!" Uhnha wept and flung her arms around him again. "May your forest always guide you to abundance."

Wolflock smiled and looked ahead of them for the

bridge they were meant to leave from. Amongst the smaller maple and pine trees along the bank, one of the strangest trees Wolflock had ever seen towered over all of them. It stood over one hundred and fifty feet high and, at a distance, it looked like an oak. But, as they drew nearer, he saw tendrils dripping from it like a green curtain.

"Ibhuloho Yomthi." Ungul stood with pride. "The Bridge Tree."

"What is it?" Wolflock scanned it with great interest.

"They say two lovers, hundreds of years ago, loved each other from opposite sides of the bank, but they could not cross, because the flighty River God Houl also loved the woman. He would destroy any ship they boarded. The man grew an oak tree, but Houl's storms smashed it. The oak tree grew back, and the woman grew a willow tree on the other side to try to join it to the oak tree. One day they finally met on that bridge. Houl was so enraged that he tore up the willow tree, but the magic of their love was too strong. The great oak and willow clung to each other, and the oak drew the willow to its side. Once united the trees wove together, making each other strong enough to continue to be a bridge for those who need it."

"But it only reaches halfway." Wolflock frowned.

"That's because when you want help you need to reach the other half of the way," Uhnha chuckled.

The sisters hugged Wolflock and Mothy one last time.

"*Kwaye vumela yakho iintolo rhoqo isiteleka nyaniso,*" Ungul hummed as she hugged Mothy. "May your arrows always strike true."

Wolflock stood back and saw her silvery tattoos glow, flowing out from her chest and stretching out down her left arm to her palm. As she drew away, she left a glowing handprint on Mothy's shirt that soaked into him.

Wolflock raised his eyebrow and smirked, catching Ungul's eye. *A blessing?*

"And you too, Mr Mischief. Thank you for your apology." Wolflock felt his chest crushed against her rock-hard muscles and her hand wrapped around the base of his skull. "*Vumela yakho amehlo rhoqo bonayo nyaniso.*"

A tingling warmth spread over the base of his head through his hair.

"What does that mean?" he asked as he drew away.

Without another word, both women scaled the rigging and took hold of the dangling vines. Wolflock ran to the starboard side of the ship and called out again as several maramuti scattered from the women climbing to a platform above. They waved back as the ship carried on away from them.

"What does that mean?!" he called out again, but no answer echoed back.

Rhiannon D. Elton

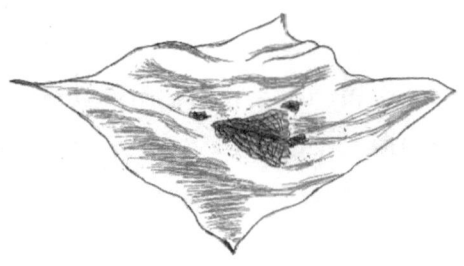

CHAPTER 2

The Blessings of Houl

The ships carried away around a bend in the river and they could see the tree no more.

"Any idea what she said?" Wolflock asked Mothy and Captain Blutro.

"I got nothin'," Mothy shrugged.

Captain Blutro just smiled and shook his head, the sound of Aujin purring mixing with his chuckle as it nestled between the back of his neck and his high collar. The silence of the early morning carried over them as they watched the sunrise creep over the opposite horizon of trees. The powdery pink light silhouetted the rousing maramuti. Every day the ship met and bid farewell to another clan of the entertaining creatures. Some were shyer than others, some were polite and mild-mannered, some were boisterous and rambunctious, while others were sneaky and mischievous. Some would swim to the boat and climb aboard, while other clans would launch themselves from the trees and try to land on the deck. For the last three days, the banks had been littered with their mud hut hovels and everyone had looked forward to seeing what the next clan's antics were like.

Over the morning, they had the luxury of dropping directly from the overhanging tuiti fruit trees. Tuiti trees were huge, standing over one hundred feet high with large mangrove-like roots and branches that stretched out as far as they could from the banks. Slavidus had told them that the trees held the river's banks together; their branches reached out so the fruit could be dropped into the river and the seeds could be dispersed downstream.

Mothy stretched his arms out wide and yawned, "I'm hungry."

"I don't think they've started breakfast yet. I haven't seen Hognut finish his pipe. It's his turn today, right, Captain?" Wolflock pinched his chin.

"Yes." Captain Blutro looked at him with a raised eyebrow. "But how did you know that?"

"Simple really. You maintain a fortnightly roster of all your crew and their duties, each one equally trained, except for Slavidus, who is only slightly less experienced than you and therefore is always on duty when you are not."

"You've been on board for nine days. How on earth did you know the roster was fortnightly when everything was in shambles for the first day you were here?"

"That was only one day before the routine resumed. You have ten crewmen plus yourself and Slavidus. The day goes in half day rosters according to set mealtimes, all of which Mothy heartily attends; breakfast, lunch, dinner, and a midnight snack. Each crewman takes care of the normal running of the ship except the chef for the meals, which gets split into two crewman's duties. It's Hognut's breakfast and lunch duty today before Goden takes over for dinner and the midnight snack shift. As I haven't seen Hognut finish his morning pipe yet, I'd say it's an accurate assumption that he hasn't started breakfast."

Captain Blutro looked impressed. "Very good, Mr Felen. I shouldn't be surprised anymore, but you still manage to catch me off my guard. I believe breakfast should be porridge with tuiti fruit. Hognut has a special method of making it even sweeter. You'll have to use those observation skills to find out though. He says it's a trade secret of his."

"I wasn't aware Hognut liked cooking."

"He doesn't like anything," Mothy chimed in. "Except for his pipe, of course."

Captain Blutro went to relieve Slavidus at the helm and the boys made tea in the kitchen as they waited for breakfast to be prepared. They chatted about what kind of lives the Blickland sisters lived back home. Mothy was particularly enthralled by their healing abilities and Wolflock remained curious about their customs and technologies.

The rest of the crew and company began meandering into the dining hall, making tea and smelling the thickly sweet smell of the porridge. Hognut would glare around the room through his bushy dark-red eyebrows and thick beard, then put his back between the diners and the cauldron, adding his next ingredient to the mix. Hognut was a large Corshman with arms as thick as trees and a chest as thick as a bull. He had red, wiry hair that wrapped around his whole head, leaving only a little gap for his eyes and nose, and no visible mouth. Wolflock and Mothy had joked in private saying that he didn't really have a mouth, but his beard absorbed all his food for him.

For Wolflock, the sticky sweet smell was overbearing. He had eaten Tuiti fruit in every way imaginable for three days and he wanted nothing more to do with it. His stomach twisted in revulsion at the smell and he sipped his bitter tea just to clear his nostrils. At one stage, he watched hopefully as Stra, a travelling herbalist, offered to share some flavourful herbs with Hognut and change things up a little. But Hognut flat out refused. Stra lingered for a few minutes as if he wanted to insist and then, to Wolflock's dismay, gave up and returned to his seat.

He must be as sick of the fruit as I am.

As it was served, Wolflock ate some bland hemp seed bread with a sour glare and pointedly pushed his portion towards Mothy.

After breakfast, everyone ventured onto the deck to get their sunshine and digest. Fuhji played a skipping and hopping game with Tinni and the two young Xiayahn boys, Gege and Didi, who were all under a decade old. Wolflock hadn't seen the boys play often, but while their father was contentedly talking to Slavidus, they were given more freedom. Wolflock and Mothy sat on some barrels by the mainmast and watched them. Wolflock noticed that there was a particular glow about Fuhji that he hadn't noticed a week ago. Her hair looked thicker and her skin had a lovely even tan to it.

"She'd make such a good ma one day. Or a good teacher," Mothy grinned, kicking his heels on the barrel.

Wolflock nodded and glanced at Froderyk, who had become far more sociable over the last few days. He was clapping along to the children's little chant and smiling from ear to ear, unable to take his loving eyes off Fuhji for even a moment.

"I wonder if they will ever have children."

"Seven months."

The voice behind Mothy was so soft and quiet that it could have been mistaken for a breeze. The Xiayahn girl, Nan Nü, had come out of the dining hall with a tray of tea for her brothers and father. Her face was rounder than those born in Grothener and her fair skin was as smooth as a babe's. Her dark, almond-shaped eyes glanced quickly away as the boys turned to her and her long black hair partitioned over her face. Wolflock had noticed that they always prepared their own food and tea, save for the nights when Grogen cooked. He'd heard their father, Nan Ji, irritably complaining that the food would affect their stomach qi. Everything he proudly proclaimed to the other passengers was always about how a good doctor never died before he reached one hundred, and that everything his children ate was to increase their longevity. Wolflock found the man to be rather self-absorbed and incapable of holding a civil conversation in which he didn't try to outdo the other person.

"Seven months? How can you tell if she's pregnant?" Wolflock demanded with an air of incredulity.

Nü bit her bottom lip and shrugged her shoulders, looking for a way past them. Her shoulders were tense, hunched up under her ears and her eyes darted back and forth at the gaps between them. Wolflock raised an eyebrow at her demeanour. Surely, he and Mothy were not threatening. Why was she nervous?

"Yes! How do you know?" Mothy interjected, but it sounded more like a strangled guffaw.

Wolflock turned to his friend to see why he sounded so off colour only to see that he was off colour. He had flushed hot pink under his straw-coloured hair.

"She has suddenly become very picky with her food and when she first boarded, she had a terrible vomiting condition." Nü glanced over to Fuhji with a hint of a smile, but suddenly her eyes went wide, and she tucked her chin down. "I mean! This is what father and Gege said. I had to examine her and found her pulse and other symptoms, but I certainly gained my conclusion from-"

"Nü!"

Her father had barked across the way, sitting up and glaring at the boys so hard his eyes had become slits of suspicion. "Guò lái!"

Without another word she bowed her head and scurried over to her father. As she walked away her lips thinned in distaste for the old man's tone, but she still silently presented him with the tea. She took her seat by him with her hands folded in her lap, but Wolflock could tell she was keeping her eyes just off them. She looked agitated and uncomfortable, fiddling with the hem of her long brown sleeves before catching herself and falling still again, just to start rolling the fabric in her fingers without realising.

"I really wanted to hear her explanation," he sighed in disappointment.

"Too me... I mean- me too!" Mothy stammered.

"She's rather lonely, isn't she?" Wolflock leaned back, soaking up more sun.

"It breaks my heart. She's such a beautiful girl. Did you know she's more trained in medicine than most doctors in Chalongesh?"

"Really? How did you find that out?" Wolflock

raised his eyebrow at Mothy's statement and his sudden coherence.

He gets flustered whenever she's near...

"Her father brags about all his children. Mostly his eldest son, but she has to treat the conditions the ladies on the ship have. He won't let his children besides her touch women for some reason."

"That is very bizarre."

Mothy let out a loud belch and held his stomach, looking very bloated.

"How many bowls did you have this morning?"

"Uhh.... About four, I think. No five! You gave me yours."

Wolflock felt like he'd be sick in sympathy to Mothy's stomach.

"I know you're giving me that look but I could have three more easily... Oh..." he belched again. "Urgh... maybe not."

Wolflock's mouth twisted in distaste.

"Now I know what you're thinking and I'm going to be fine. Not even a temperature, see?" He pulled Wolflock's hand to his forehead. "I..." he trailed off and his eyes homed in on something moving across the deck and to the stairs below deck. Wolflock followed his line of sight and saw a head of smooth black hair descend to the cabins. Mothy scratched the back of his head.

"...Maybe.... You're right. I'm going to see if... a lay down will help. I'll come back later."

It's not even mid-morning, Wolflock thought.

"Good chat, Lockie. I'll be back for lunch."

And, with that, he was gone. Wolflock sighed and leaned back on the mast, watching the banks for more maramuti as the passengers chatted. Grogen chased one of the maramuti around the deck after it took his spoon and the children stopped their game to laugh at their antics. Although the morning was filled with frivolity, there was a distinct sense that something was missing.

The Blickland sisters.

Their presence had been so fundamental to the ship that, without them there, the atmosphere was lacking. As Grogen recovered his spoon triumphantly, the maramuti hanging off the back of his shirt, Wolflock thought of how, when he finished his studies, he and Mothy could travel and visit the Blickland sisters and have their questions answered about their lifestyle and customs.

"Alright, children," Fuhji sang. "We must stop stirring the maramuti or they'll misbehave. We must show them good behaviour so Grogen needs not to fear for his spoon."

They all laughed and bounced up to Fuhji.

"First mate, Mr Slavidus, is going to tell us a story now. Would you all like to hear a story?"

"Yes, Miss Kor-sa-ki," they chanted in unison. Grogen, with ten times more enthusiasm, roared with them, causing another round of giggles.

"Well, take a seat and we will get started."

Slavidus cleared his throat and took a breath.

"Once upon a time there was no river here. The land was soft and ran along a ley line, so of course the magic of the land began to fill it up. As when magic comes together, it brings forth the elements. The element of water won the space first though and all the creatures rejoiced because they knew that water brought life. Plants grew, fish came, and animals drank the water, but it kept on flowing, all the way from the sea in the North to the ocean in the South.

The creatures loved this river so much, but one creature, the rabbit, listened to the river and loved it more than any other. The rabbit listened so carefully that one day it heard the river's voice.

"Oh, little one," it said through its rumbling waters, "you who listens to me so well, who eats the plants that flow beyond their borders, who runs alongside me every day. I am Houl, God of this river."

And the rabbit who was humbled by the great waters said, "Oh, mighty one, who nurtures this land, how might I serve you?"

"You have done all I could ask for. I only wish to bless you with a gift. Ask of me anything within my power and I shall grant it."

And on that day the rabbit asked to be able to act as the river's guardian forever more. Houl turned it into the Reedbit we know today."

Wolflock smiled. He'd heard this story before. Reedbits were green, algae covered rabbit-looking creatures with ears that looked like seaweed and webbed feet instead of paws. They shot themselves through the water with bursts of speed aided by their powerful back legs.

"And it is from the Reedbits that sailors are taught how to respect our river. Reedbits never bring foreign items into the water. They do their toilet business on the banks. They drag their dead or injured onto the land. They run away from creatures rather than kill them in the water. Their skin shrivels if it's touched by drinking alcohol, so we never touch it either.

Reedbits are the messengers, the eyes and ears of Houl. Never should a sailor disrespect him. Never shall we break his laws. If we honour the river, we will be blessed with a safe journey."

"What happens if someone does break the laws?" Tinni asked in awe of the tale.

"Houl cannot see into ships, so when someone on a ship breaks one of his laws, he curses the whole ship."

The children gasped and huddled closer.

"What does he do?" Gege whispered.

"Sometimes, he sinks the ship by crashing it onto rocks. Sometimes, he makes all the food go bad and the sailors must leave the water. Sometimes he stops the flow of the river so the ship travels poorly, and, sometimes, he makes everyone on board so ill that they-"

"Whoa, Slavidus!" Captain Blutro hollered from the helm. "Don't get the children frightened now. We want them to be able to sleep tonight."

"My apologies, Captain. It's very easy to stay in Houl's good books, children. Don't throw anything off the ship that doesn't belong in the river. Be as well behaved as you have been and Houl will continue to bless us with delicious food, great entertainment from the animals, and strong winds to keep us sailing."

Wolflock hopped off his barrel and walked away as Froderyk and Fuhji quickly distracted the children, resuming their skipping game. He recalled the tales of the local North Grothien gods of the forest, like Miulukki the

Huntress who appeared as a deer and guarded the forests, and Adelar the Watchful, a great golden eagle who maintained a balance between the skies and land. He wanted to tell Mothy about them and how they were like the river god Houl with their protection of a natural environment. But his friend had not yet returned. Without Mothy, the lustre of the ship's company evaporated, and he decided to stroll about the deck. The aft of the ship was currently being used as a laundry space, with empty lines ready for the midday wash. The laundry would be collected during lunch, new sheets would be placed on the beds, and the old laundry would be washed along with some essential clothing items.

It surprised Wolflock to see a piece of cloth flickering in the breeze on the lid of one of the washing barrels. He caught the small white handkerchief on a splinter and had traces of a herbal powder and what looked like a small chunk of dark purple jerky caught on it.

Was this someone's snack?

Recalling the story of how Houl didn't like his river filled with foreign objects, he picked up the cloth and pocketed it before it could blow away. He finished his turn about the ship when he saw Mothy return to the deck, looking sheepish.

"Your stomach feeling better?"

"Huh? Oh. Yes. A lay down was all I needed." He scratched his chin, shrugging his shoulders.

Wolflock had promised to give Mothy his privacy when he chose to keep things to himself, but he couldn't help but feel a little stung that there was something he clearly wasn't sharing with him.

"Lunch will be ready soon," Goden shouted as he collected tuiti fruit from the deck in a barrel under his burly arm.

Wolflock pulled a face, but it gave Goden fuel to round on him.

"Sorry, your highness, but you'll be grateful we have so much flavour when we hit the Hatfjorn Lake. Nothing but fish, salt and preserves out there."

"Oh goodie. Can't wait," Wolflock drawled.

Goden leaned in close with a mean grin. "I'll let Hognut know to serve yeh up his biggest bowl tonight because yeh like it s'much!"

Wolflock suspected that they would be having more tuiti soup for lunch. The sun was at its peak when his suspicions were confirmed, and Hognut grumpily brought out a pot of soup.

"Grubs up!" he announced to a hungry company.

Everyone gathered their bowls and spoons as the

crew ate some of the fruit raw, waiting for their turn. Wolflock chose to just have hemp seed bread while Mothy ate three bowls to himself as well as everyone else's leftovers when he offered to help clean up.

"Yours is wriggling!" Tinni giggled and pointed at Hognut's beard as it consumed a very soft and chewy tuiti fruit.

Suddenly, Hognut began spluttering and threw it over the side of the ship.

"What's wrong?" Slavidus frowned.

"It's a river bug larva!"

The crew collectively grew pale.

"What's a river bug?" Wolflock looked around, expecting a response from the crew.

"It's the larvae of a type of crustacean that is camouflaged to look like the tuiti fruit so that the fish in the water don't eat it. Tuiti fruit are poisonous to the fish until their skin has broken down. The River Bugs are very poisonous to us though," Captain Blutro answered solemnly. "You can tell which is which because tuiti fruit float. Rive Bugs don't."

"Hognut! You didn't put any in the soup, did you?" Slavidus demanded.

Hognut's beard looked mightily offended.

"I ain't dumb!" he scoffed "I chop 'em up good

and proper before I chuck 'em in the pot!"

"Aye, aye. I was only asking. Calm your bald head. Geagle, go check the barrels." Slavidus shushed him and sat back down.

Although the lunch was safe, Wolflock's gut still told him he'd best stick to the bland bread rather than any more sickly-sweet fruit.

He turned to Mothy, who was beginning to look very ill.

"You didn't eat one, did you?" Wolflock's brow furrowed, believing his friend would eat anything.

"Nay..." Mothy groaned and struggled to smile, "I just... bleh... ate too much..."

"Goden, please tell us we have something different for dinner," Wolflock moaned.

"You'll eat what's given to yeh and be grateful for it!" Goden brandished his spoon under Wolflock's nose.

"Ah... whoops!" He pretended to lean on the table and put his hand on the edge of a half full bowl and splashed it all down Goden's leg and onto the floor.

"Why you-"

"Look out!" Mothy cried as Veluse slipped in the soup on the floor, flinging his lukewarm bowl all over Mothy.

Mothy blinked through the soup, licked his lips,

and scooped it off his face. Then he mushed it onto Wolflock's face. Wolflock recoiled and mashed it back onto Mothy, who retaliated in kind, flicking chunks of fruit at his friend, who ducked and let the pieces splatter all over Tanni. Tinni plunged her hand into her mother's bowl and threw soup at Didi.

And it was on.

They hurled soup and fruit all over the deck and, when people ran out of soup in their bowls, they ran for the cauldron to get more. Goden tried to grab the boys but only managed to grab Mothy's shirt collar.

"Mind my shirt thanks, Goden."

The slippery boy dropped out of his oversized shirt and ran around the deck topless, dodging incoming fruit even more effectively than when he was clothed. Everyone but Goden and Nan Ji were in fits of laughter. At one point someone threw a whole tuiti fruit at Yifi, but Slavidus heroically launched himself between the two and laid winded on the deck.

Finally, Captain Blutro bellowed across the ship and the captain deemed the boys the instigators. He made them swab the whole deck and set them to do laundry all afternoon.

As the afternoon grew from blue to orange, the boys scrubbed the sheets and all the fruit stained clothes.

But they had fun talking and reminiscing about the afternoon and their best shots. Mothy's movements started to slow down and his belches became more frequent as they got closer to the bottom of the washing basket.

"You're not looking so good there."

"You know, all that running and how much I ate has not left my gut in a good place."

"Could have also been the under-ripe tuiti that hit you square in the stomach."

"Aye... thanks for that by the way."

Wolflock chuckled, pinning up another shirt.

"Go on. I'll finish these. If you have some tea, it might settle it down."

"Mmmm.... Maybe the Nan family has a good tea for it. See you at dinner."

Wolflock nodded and let him go. In the short time he'd known Mothy, Wolflock had developed a deep appreciation for his company. He was kind, generous and seemed to think of the things that were overlooked. For the present time, Wolflock had a use for Mothy, but there was also a degree of sentimental attachment that he had only ever felt for his immediate family.

He finished the laundry, his arms heavy and sore, and flopped on the deck among the waving sheets. The clouds blended in with the white cloths easily and the sun felt like warm hands on his face, drying the water. As he closed his eyes and relaxed into a doze, he had a final thought about his friend.

Mothy must be my brother in spirit. It will be fun to venture to Mystentine with him and hopefully... all around the world...

CHAPTER 3
Surely, It's Nothing

*ngh!"*

Wolflock scrunched his face. Someone was touching his hair.

"*Blergh!*"

Splash.

Wolflock blinked his eyes open and sat up, his muscles aching from laying on the hard deck for so long. A tiny fluffy ball rolled off Wolflock's black hair, and he glanced around to see the baby maramuti that had been grooming him. The sky was pink from the setting sun, shadowing the bulky figure leaning over the taffrail. The figure retched again.

"Grogen?"

"Wolflo-*blergh*?"

The huge man slumped back over the railing and released his stomach into the river with a horrendous splash. As Wolflock approached, he saw something floating in the water away from the ship.

A jacket? Had one blown off? He shook his head and turned back to Grogen.

"Isn't it bad form for a crewman to be getting seasick?"

Grogen glared back at him irritably before spitting out watery vomit and slumping down the ground.

"Hush, boy!" he croaked. "I ain't got seasick. This... this is... is sumthin' else..."

"What makes you say that?" he frowned.

Grogen sighed, spat again and turned around, leaning against the baluster.

"I only got seasick for a 'alf moon when I first joined the crew. I was a youngin' and I didn't 'ave me ship legs. Plus," he added and raised his huge trembling hands in front of him, "I ain't never got the shakes like this unless we been in Shiriling in Winter, but I'm fryin' up!"

Wolflock stared curiously at his hands, bulky and

hairy. They were quivering as if he was freezing.

"I'm all hot and I'm shiverin'. None of it makes no sense!" groaned the huge man, holding his stomach.

"Why not speak to Nan Ji? Isn't he a medical practitioner?"

Grogen got wobbly to his feet and took a breath, "Aye... aye... that's what I'll do... Where would 'e be, boy?"

Wolflock was confused by his question. Surely, he should know that it's dinnertime...

"In the dining hall, I suppose?" he offered. "Do you want me to get him for you?"

"Nah... nah... Aye... Aye...I'll go..."

Wolflock walked cautiously beside the crewman as he stumbled to the dining hall. As they entered, Wolflock surveyed the room for Mothy, but saw that his friend, Slavidus, Yifi, Hognut and Parihaan were all absent. He could only guess why Slavidus and Yifi were missing together. Ever since his second day on the ship, they had become better friends. Hognut was probably sleeping as he was on the breakfast shift in the morning, and Parihaan left early most nights and was late to any events. But he had no idea why Mothy was not present.

His stomach might still be sore.

Goden was serving Tanni and Tinni their bowls of

Tuiti fruit stew and Wolflock felt his stomach churn.

"I 'ope it's to yah likin'. I tried a few new 'erbs but I canna' smell so good n'more."

"Is there anything else to eat?" Wolflock cut in, keeping Grogen in his peripheries as he asked Nan Ji about a treatment.

"Not until we run out of Tuiti fruit." Goden's stubbly face broke into a wicked grin. "Now quit yer belly achin' and don' waste it!"

Wolflock scowled as he took the smallest bowl of the stew and snatched up a whole loaf of hemp seed bread. He proceeded to sit down at the dining table and tore a bite out of the bread, sighing at the quickly dwindling company. Everyone leaving looked a bit green.

They're probably sick of the fruit too...

He tried to look at the stew but, as he poked the fluorescent pink and green chunks with his spoon, his stomach shirked away, demanding savoury foods or nothing at all. Eventually he looked around and reseated next to Veluse, Fuhji, Geagle and the twins, Faleen and Bleen.

"Where is everyone tonight?"

Veluse leaned back dramatically and swept his hand to his brow. "Oh woe, poor boy! You've not heard?"

Wolflock's face went flat. Veluse's antics used to be mildly funny, but he had long grown tired of the artist's theatrics, particularly when he just wanted a simple question answered.

"No," he drawled. "Pray, tell me what has them missing another scrumptious dinner."

It was more of a command than a request. He wanted to know more about Mothy's state than the others.

"Oh, woe to them! Poor, poor souls! Poor, poor, poor, poor troubled souls."

Wolflock refused to feed into the man's drama and simply waited. But, as he expected, Veluse continued without answering the question.

"You should have seen them. You really should have. You might have been able to help. Those poor, poor darlings. There was nothing I could do, you see. They just all... oh it was wretched!"

"Veluse," Wolflock hissed through gritted teeth, "Why is Mothy not here?!"

Veluse began to chuckle, satisfied. "Oh, dear boy! I didn't know you had such strong... feelings for your friend!"

"If you'll not answer my questions, I'll go and find him for myself!" he snapped and rose from the table.

"Mothy never made it to dinner," Fuhji answered, breaking away from her conversation with the twins as she rolled a raw tuiti fruit in her hands. Her husband was eating his bowl and hers with feverish vigour.

"Oh?"

"He went downstairs not long after lunch and hasn't emerged since. The captain says he is ill. Slavidus too. And Parihaan."

"Thank you, Fuhji," Wolflock nodded, his temper dropping as he rose to his feet, collecting his bowl of stew for Mothy with his bread still gripped in his right hand.

"...now Grogen too... this is not good. This is not good..." Geagle began to rock back and forth. His watery blue eyes staring dead ahead. "Oh no... oh no..."

Everyone stopped and stared at him.

"What are you mumbling?" Wolflock asked.

"Houl... Houl may have... cursed us," his voice dropped lower with every word until it was barely a whisper.

The effect on the room was sudden. The twins both backed their chairs up in horror, Veluse and Fuhji grasped their hearts. Froderyk and Wolflock just frowned.

"Why ever would you say that?" Wolflock leaned on his left leg and tapped his.

"We're all getting sick. Grogen never gets sick. This is a bad omen... We've done somethin'k that displeases Houl!"

For a large, fully grown large man, Wolflock always thought Geagle looked quite pitiful. Droopy blue eyes, very little chin and thin blonde hair that was bound to leave him bald one day. That, along with his bland conversation purely about ships and ladies, Wolflock had dismissed any future communication with him entirely. This was the most interesting he had been since Plugh, although Wolflock nearly retracted the thought when he put a 'k' sound on the end of 'something'.

"That's ludicrous," Froderyk snorted. "Besides Fuhji, Mothy is the most delightful person on the ship. Houl wouldn't curse him!"

"Oi!" Goden barked from the kitchen. "None of that now!"

The burly beardless crewman thumped over and put a fist on the table between Geagle and the others.

"I can 'ear yeh from the kitchen. None of that talk. Houl is good to us. He doesn't curse us, and I don' wan' ta se yeh trying to rile 'im up! Now no more word on it."

Geagle continued to rock, not making eye contact, stirring his food slowly. "Houl isn't picky... he can't see onto the ship. He doesn't know anyone's face on here."

"I said enough!"

Wolflock rolled his eyes and walked away before he had to hear anymore. Superstitious origins to an illness were as rare as hen's teeth as far as he was concerned and there had been no great insult to the river that would warrant such wrath. If Geagle had no proof, then he had no desire to listen to him.

As he descended the stairs, he saw Nan Ji leading Grogen down to the crew's sleeping quarters with a lidded pot of medicine. He could hear the mournful groans of Parihaan down the hall, but only an eerie silence emanated from Mothy's room.

"Mothy?" he asked and opened his friend's door. "Are you awake?"

To his surprise, Mothy laid flat on his back with his bed neatly wrapped around him. His eyes were closed, but, even in the dim fairy lantern light, his skin looked damp and washed out.

"Aye..." he groaned and opened his eyes. As Wolflock approached, he could see that the normal glittering grey blue had changed to a dull and cloudy shade.

"I brought you food. Fuhji told me you hadn't been up to dinner."

"Oh, thank you!" he croaked and propped himself

up as if he ached all over. "I've never travelled this far North before. I think the air is affecting me..."

Wolflock smiled and sat on the edge of his bed, giving him the spoon and bowl, before biting into the bland nutty bread. He couldn't help but notice that Mothy started sweating and, as he ate, his hand trembled enough to spill out half of its contents.

"You're feeling ill, aren't you? You look it."

"Bloody awful..." he said through a mouthful of stew. "I'm hot and cold and my stomach is trying to climb out my face."

Wolflock took another bite, frowning. He didn't know anything about medicine or healing.

I should be able to learn more about herbs and medicines at Mystentine.

"Hopefully the food will settle it all down."

"Mmm..."

"Tell me a story, Lockie?"

Wolflock laughed, but as he looked at Mothy, who had snuggled back down into his sheets, he could only see sincerity in his face.

"Very well... Mother used to tell me this one just after Myna was born. Once upon a Springtime there was a little sprout. The tiny sprout was so new and green, but it couldn't grow big and strong because the winds blew it around and the rain was too heavy. One day a boulder rolled over it and said,

"Little tree, I see you need help. I will stay with you and keep you safe."

The tree was very thankful, and one day grew into a mighty strong tree that no wind could blow down, and no flood could threaten. By that time, though, the rock had grown old and had begun to crumble away.

"Oh, my little tree," the rock spoke. "I am afraid I will soon be no more."

And the tree replied, "You were so kind and helped me when I was a sapling. You kept me safe and allowed me to grow strong and tall. I will now do the same for you."

And with that the tree pulled up half of its roots from the ground and wrapped them around the rock, forever holding it together. And they still live happily ever after."

As he spoke, Wolflock saw Mothy's face looked less peaky and his eyes had gotten some of their sparkle back. By the time he finished his story, Mothy was fast asleep.

As Wolflock climbed into bed, he wrote to his sister again, not because he had anything to say, but because he hoped to hear Mothy's snores start up and let him know that his friend would get back to normal soon.

Rhiannon D. Elton

CHAPTER 4
The Mysterious Illness

"H*ngh!*"

Wolflock's face scrunched up as a noise roused him from his slumber.

"*Blergh!*"

He felt the warmth of the blanket around his slender frame and was convinced he was still dreaming until he heard a chunky splash. The noise made him feel sick, but it wasn't coming from Mothy's room. It seemed to come from Haatji's room across the hallway.

"I have your hair, Haatji. Didi, empty her bucket," came Nü's soft voice, followed by the tiny footsteps of the smallest brother.

Wolflock didn't want to move. The grey Autumn light of the morning felt cold and dreary, but his curiosity got the better of him when he heard a flump sound from Mothy's room next to him.

Wolflock sat up and realised why he was so cold. An adolescent maramuti was sitting in his open porthole window, biting into a raw potato and swinging its long flat ended tail inside the cabin.

"Can I help?" Mothy croaked and Wolflock sat up to see him drag his feet limply toward Haatji's room.

Haatji was shaking her head and looked pale even under her olive skin.

"She doesn't want a man to touch her," Nü said softly and touched Mothy's shoulder as she reached above Haatji's bed to get a towel.

Her touch had such a profound effect on Mothy that it startled Wolflock into full alertness. Mothy stood up straight with his chest pushed out and then fainted on the spot. Wolflock leaped forward, his blanket caught around one leg and rushed to his friend.

"Oh, dear!" Nü gasped as she pressed into a point on Haatji's wrist and tried to reach for Mothy, too. "Wolflock. Please take Mothy back to bed. I'm the only one who can tend to Haatji."

Wolflock had caught Mothy from hitting his head on the floor and nodded to Nü, dragging his unconscious friend back onto his bed that was still abnormally neat, with the sheets folded back.

His head was clear now and his brain had fully engaged. Mothy was in a terrible state and he knew he could help; he just wasn't sure how.

"What can I do?" he asked quickly as Haatji lost consciousness.

Nü looked at him as they both heard another bout of vomiting from Dlumi's room. Her porcelain face was oddly calm, reminding Wolflock of some of his strictest tutors.

"Father may need you. He's with Slavidus. I'm helping Haatji because only women can touch her. We need buckets though."

"Is there anything I can do for Mothy?" he asked, concern etched across his sharp features.

"Make sure he doesn't stand again and keep one bucket of water as well as one empty bucket near him. We need two for each. Haatji has one already."

Wolflock couldn't tell if she knew she could trust him to know why she needed them, or if she didn't think he'd comprehend it. He frowned, wondering if she was intelligent enough to perceive his mental acuity, or if he'd have to make it more obvious in the future. With all this vomiting, it was essential that they maintained their fluids. He hastily dressed into his slacks, shoes and shirt, and dashed downstairs into the crew's quarters. As he dashed between the two rows of hammocks to grab the buckets, he saw Nü's middle brother, Gege, trying to stand under the enormous weight of the crewman Groger.

"P-please lay back down! You're not well enough to stand Mr Groger!" he squeaked, his legs trembling under the six-foot-tall boulder of a man.

"I... I need to... need to... the ship..." he wheezed before he collapsed.

Gege would have been crushed had Wolflock not darted forward and helped him to catch the falling giant.

"Bed!" Gege gasped as he began dragging Groger to the bedding that had fallen under his hammock.

Wolflock nodded and helped heave the huge man onto his back on the undersized makeshift bed. Gege grabbed a towel from the cabinet at the head of his hammock to wipe the sweat and vomit off him.

"Have you seen my father?" Gege panted as he patted down Groger's face with the cleaner end of the cloth.

"He's treating Slavidus in the first mate's room, I expect. Do you need anything else? Did you want me to get your father?" Wolflock asked, wanting to get away from the sick in case he caught what they had.

"Thank the moon someone is tending to him! No, no! Please don't tell-I mean don't worry him. If you see him, let him know everything is fine. Where is Nü?" Gege's voice quavered.

"With Haatji and Dlumi upstairs. What's wrong with them?"

Gege looked fearfully at Goden, who was turning his head and mumbling a delirious string of nonsense.

"I do not know... N-I mean, father will know! Father will know for sure. I need a bucket of water to cool him, please and thank you!"

Wolflock realised three things. One, it was obvious that Gege didn't want his father to see him struggling. Two, he was very inexperienced at his father's craft. Three, he needed an extra bucket to catch any befoulment that Goden may spew out.

Wolflock was already scanning the ship according to his observations from yesterday, locating the closest buckets that had most likely not been moved. He knew that he needed seven buckets. Two for Mothy, one extra for Haatji, two for Dlumi and two for Groger. He also didn't understand why Gege was by himself when, clearly, he was nervous and not apt at healing.

It mustn't be a crisis. That's what that means. If Nan Ji is such a good practitioner, he would have known he couldn't send in an amateur.

He ran downstairs into the hull and found four wooden buckets with rough hemp rope handles, each filled with dried fruit that he promptly tipped out into another barrel. He hooked his arm through them all and ran upstairs, not knowing when or where the next bout of vomiting would occur. As he ran to the cabin stairs, he hastily dropped a bucket by Groger and Gege.

"I need water in it," he called out as Wolflock dashed past.

He found another two buckets with mops in them at the base of the stairs. The mops fell with a clatter, but, in his urgency, Wolflock didn't care. He left three of the buckets at the room that Nü was in and shoved Mothy back into bed as he tried to climb back out. As he ran onto the deck and used a loose rope to drop the remaining buckets into the freshwater river. He was one bucket short, though, which he realised when he had filled the first three. He scanned the deck, but only found half a barrel of tuiti fruit, which he happily tipped out and filled with the water he'd gotten from his last bucket before refilling it.

Finally, having four containers with water he began

lugging them downstairs, first one to Mothy, who he had to threaten with a fierce glare to get to lay down again, then two for Nü to hand out and the last to Gege.

"Oh! I had not thought of that!" the young boy exclaimed with a tired, happy sigh.

Not used to doing such strenuous physical labour, Wolflock's arms ached, and his initial adrenaline had worn off. He was now tired and hungry, and the sun had barely risen. He needed food.

"I'm going to get breakfast, Miss Nü. Let me know if there are any updates on Mothy," he groaned as he approached the Dlumi's room.

It surprised him to see Nü jump away from her patient and tuck one arm behind her back, looking startled. Dlumi was sweating, but she didn't seem as delirious or shaky as the others.

Is it her robust Corshwoman nature? Perhaps the illness is about to resolve.

"Um. Ah. No. No, that is all thanks. Father may want some assistance though. He is in Slavidus' room. I will come and get you when I need aid if that is good." Her voice shook a little but Wolflock was too hungry to pay it much heed. Her accent was very pleasant though. She said her words in a different part of her mouth, making it sound like a bubbling brook.

"Aye," he huffed in response as he slumped away.

Now that he was fully awake and he had averted any messy crisis, Wolflock felt above the position of errand boy or bucket collector and wished to resign to the dining hall. But, regardless, he made his way to Slavidus' room and knocked twice before entering.

Nan Ji was taking Slavidus' pulse and Yifi stood by the door glaring, twisting a handkerchief in her hands.

"Yifi?" Wolflock queried, not wanting to disturb Nan Ji or be given anymore chores that didn't directly affect Mothy's health. "What are you doing here?"

Yifi growled and dropped her voice, "I came to help and see if there was something I could do, but Nan Ji is one of those men... He won't let me do a thing!"

"Why not?" Wolflock frowned, thinking if Yifi could help, then he could go and eat.

"Because I'm a woman..."

Wolflock was confused. "What do you mean? Is this a gender-based illness?"

"No. It's just a cold. But he believes women are not capable or intelligent."

Wolflock didn't think men anywhere in the world still clung to those ridiculous ideals anymore. Thinking that either sex could be lesser in any way made no sense to him, and the vast majority of men in Puinteyle treasured women, for it was by a woman that they were created. Everyone knew that even the very Earth was feminine, for she birthed all life, so to denounce women was nearly to denounce life itself.

For a thousand years the royal family had promoted balance between the sexes, nations and cultures of all people, so hearing that Nan Ji wouldn't allow a woman to assist him sounded preposterous. Especially when Yifi was quite a clever and capable lady. There was also the fact that his daughter was a trained physician and appeared to be quite adept.

Or does he not know his daughter is practicing? Does he just ignore it? Surely no one could be that obtuse.

"It is because she does not know what this complex medicine needs!" Nan Ji retorted hotly and dropped Slavidus' arm. "Women's brains are not big enough to comprehend the complexities that are associated with healing!"

His heated words seemed even more obnoxious and absurd as they came from the small man with his thick Xiayahn accent and red face. Wolflock just rolled his eyes.

"Well, I've just spent my morning hauling buckets for vomiting passengers. I'm fairly sure Yifi is just as apt at that as I am."

"Do not give me cheek, little boy!" said the short angry man. "Gege would have instructed you for all those buckets with good reason! One for the sick, one for their hydration. You are to go about his orders as instructed without complaint!"

"It wasn't Gege. It was Nü who sent me. Gege only wanted water buckets," Wolflock blinked and felt his anger bubbling hotter.

"Pfft!" the old man dismissed him, "The girl probably listened to Gege and repeated his instructions. She knows she is only to report the symptoms of the females. Not diagnose or give instruction. Go and have food, little boy. Clearly, you spoke with Gege and his brilliant mind confused you-"

"Yifi...." Slavidus groaned and reached out an aching arm to the beautiful lady.

She smiled and stepped forward before Wolflock could begin yelling at Nan Ji.

"If you've finished your treatment, I'm happy to watch him." She smiled and held his hand to her cheek.

Nan Ji pursed his lips and glared at the two of them before storming out, swearing in his native tongue.

"Don't make him too mad, Master Felen," Slavidus croaked. "He's a wizard with herbs, and he can make you ill if you aren't careful."

"Duly noted."

"Do you feel better after his medicine?" Yifi simpered.

Slavidus smiled at her, his eyes glassy and his skin translucent. "We have to be careful. Someone has done something to enrage Houl. I've never seen him curse a ship like this."

"It can't be!" She frowned and squeezed his hand. "It's just a cold. Don't be silly."

"It's just like Captain's father..."

"Captain said you're not to talk about that, remember? It's not to do with any of that. Now you rest. I'm going to get you some more food and drink."

Wolflock took his queue to leave with her and headed to the dining hall for a well-deserved breakfast.

The sun was completely visible now and was quite warm against the brisk chill of the morning air. He was sorely disappointed when he smelt the sickly-sweet smell of more tuiti fruit being cooked in the ship's oven.

Surely it couldn't be a curse. You have to do horrendous things in order for something as strong as a god to curse you... There has to be a rational explanation, Wolflock thought as he sat down.

Goden was singing happily as he cooked, oblivious that the company at the breakfast table was significantly less than their normal eighteen or more.

"Eat up, Master Felen!" he grinned and gave him a small wooden plate of sliced baked fruit.

Wolflock scowled at Goden and snatched up another hemp seed loaf, taking his meal out onto the deck to enjoy the sun. He needed the fresh air.

The web of this sudden illness began to form in his mind. At the centre was the illness. Each thread attached was a person. Mothy, Grogen, Slavidus, Groger, Haatji, Dlumi, Parihaan. They each would have had to have interacted with a common point to get and spread the illness. That is where their threads would rejoin but surrounding them was the unlikely chance that Houl had cursed the ship and it was spreading. He pinched his chin with one hand and reached into his pocket with the other, rolling around the white handkerchief he'd picked up earlier.

What were the common factors that linked them all? Surely it couldn't be as simple of an angry god. The gods at home were only ever offended by tremendous disrespect to their habitats and traditions.

The ship was a small place, so proximity was always a danger, but everyone had interacted with all other members at some stage. Who was ill first though? What did they come into contact with? How could he find the answers?

"Uh... Mr Felen, sir?"

Wolflock jumped in alarm and looked on the intruder with distaste. Geagle wiped his nose on his sleeve and hesitantly made eye contact.

"I... um... I was hopin' you'd... well... Can you use your smarts to see why we've upset Houl? Maybe if we fix it, he'll take away the sickness."

"Don't be foolish, man. It's just a cold."

"But it ain't!" he whined, twisting his fingers. "It ain't just a sickness! Grogen never gets sick. And now Slavidus, too. I even saw the twins going green and Cap'in too! Everyone is gonna die and I just... I just thought..."

Wolflock sighed, rolling his eyes. "What have you got to make it worth my while? I can mostly definitely prove to you this isn't a curse from the river god, and that it is merely a sickness from a very ordinary source, but it's such a droll chore. What have you got that could entertain me?"

Geagle nodded and opened a pouch on his belt. "This was Charice's puzzle book that she gave me to make me cleverer. I can't figure it out and we're over now, so I don' want the reminder."

Wolflock flicked through the puzzle book and saw a few tricky number games he liked the look of. "Deal."

"Oh, thank you, Mr Wolflock! Thank you! I know you'll be able to save her-er. Them! Thank you!"

"I was going to figure it out anyway, but what makes you think this is a curse?"

"Gro-"

"Besides Grogen being ill. Yes, I heard that. Surely the river god is not so fickle."

"Well... I... Umm..."

"Why would Houl curse a ship? Especially one that has thus far been very respectful of his waters."

"Don't you 'ave your own gods with strict rules back in Plugh? Don't they start hurting people when they're upset?"

"Of course, they do. Every god of the land does. It takes a severe insult to their elements though, such as burning down a large portion of a forest or creating too much smog in the air. My question is: what causes Houl to curse a ship? Captain said it was throwing things into the river that don't belong there. It all seems a bit flippant to me. What else?"

"The river's delicate. Moves faster. So Houl has to be on guard faster. He's very protective of his waters and banks. What doesn't he like though? Umm..." Grogen started counting on his stumpy fingers. "Crapping in the water when you're deathly diseased."

Wolflock shook his head, taken aback. "That's disgusting. If I were a river god, I'd certainly curse a ship too if someone befouled my waters. Carry on."

"Dumping bodies without proper funeral rights, but also if the body is cursed or died from disease. Basically, if it kills the fish or plants, don't put it in the water. Transporting booze or killing wildlife that's been friendly too."

"And have you seen anyone commit these crimes?"

Geagle flushed pink, "N-n-no, sir, Mr Wolflock."

"Are you sure?"

"Yessir!"

"Well, that certainly won't help the investigation... Oh dear. I guess I'm at a complete and utter loss." Wolflock paused and waited, trying to hold back a smirk.

It only took a second.

"What do you need for your search? I'll get it for you! Anything to lift the curse!"

Wolflock clapped him on the back. "Good man. I'll need the ship's cargo log. We are going to go through this step by step, Geagle. We'll check to see if anything significant has been thrown off the side of the ship. Then bodies. Since everybody is present and alive, it means someone would have had to have brought a corpse on. The cargo log will tell us if someone has brought drinking alcohol on and, later, I'll scour the ship for any injured or dead animals. I need you to answer a few questions for me. Where is the waste kept on board?"

"If it ain't food scraps and it doesn't melt into the water or the fish's bellies, it's kept in the hull. That's what Captain always says. When we dock, the rubbish is taken ashore to be dealt with."

"And what about befouled excrement?"

"What about what now?"

Wolflock's nose wrinkled in distaste for the words about to cross his tongue.

"Crap. Particularly, crap from the sick. Where is that kept?"

"Oh! Why didn't yah just speak normal then? That's kept in a big tank in the hull that gets emptied and cleaned at certain ports. Most of the time, though, people is healthy, and it just goes in the river."

"Good to know. While you get me the cargo log, I'm going to have a look around down-"

"Oh! Captain said no one but the crew and the Nan family can go down in the hull. He doesn't want anyone touching their herbs without permission."

Wolflock looked at him with a flat stare.

"S-sorry, Mr Wolflock, sir. Captain's orders."

He drew a breath and stood up straight. "I'll just have to let the Nan family help me then."

Geagle stood there, scratching his head, trying to make sense of the Wolflock's final sentence. As he walked away, he developed a new plan. He'd offer his assistance to the Nan family to retrieve their herbs, and that would grant him permission to view the hull. If he was in the hull, obviously searching for items or dead animals, that would give any guilty parties an opportunity to hide their misdeeds or dispose of them over the ship, and he couldn't let that happen. Not if he was going to prove that a river god would not be so flippant or attempting to injure Mothy. Just as he got to the stairs, he heard the dining hall door bang and three maramuti started 'hroo hroo'ing. Nü had a tray of herbal concoctions that the strange creatures desperately wanted.

"Get away! Get away!"

Perfect timing, he thought as he began shooing the creatures from her legs and one from her shoulder. That one firmly placed itself on his shoulder instead.

"Thank you. I did not know if I would make it passed them. They like my herbs as much as our patients have," Nü smiled and relaxed her shoulders.

"Do you know what the cause of the illness is yet?" he asked, matching her step and keeping the maramuti at bay, gently pushing the maramuti on his shoulder hand's down.

Nü shook her head. "I wish I did. We are a lot further from home than I would like. The diseases and herbs are all very different. I am glad I can help, though."

"You're a natural healer, aren't you?" Wolflock pushed the one on his shoulders hand's down again.

Nü blushed. "Oh no. You are mistaken. My brother is the better healer. I just do what he and father say."

"Was anyone sick before Plugh?" He pushed the maramuti's hand down once more.

"No. Everyone was fit and healthy, for the most part. I have seen a similar sickness before. Normally, it passes after two days and with lots of fluids. As long as no one starts vomiting blood, they are safe."

Something in her words itched at Wolflock. If she wasn't a healer, how would she know about Fuhji's pregnancy? Or about how this sickness would progress? He pushed the maramuti's hand back down as he kept in step with Nü. "I would like to help. I want Mothy to get well as quickly as possible."

Nü's face brightened. "I would appreciate that. Father says that I may treat the women, but, sometimes, he forgets herbs that are better for women. You could get them for me. I am not permitted to touch them."

"Geagle said all of your family had permission to go down to collect herbs."

"Permission from the Captain, yes. But father has said I may not."

"That's ridiculous! You know the herbs you need, aye? Is your father an imbecile? People are sick and he wants to get them well with a hand tied behind his back merely to uphold some outdated ideologies?"

"No! He just-"

"Nü!" barked the small man from the entrance of the stairs. "What are you doing? Those herbs are only useful when hot. Get them to my patients!"

She bowed her head and scampered down the stairs, something glittering in her hair that Wolflock didn't quite grab the image of. Nan Ji came up the stairs and made sure to stand two steps above the young man, bringing him to just above eye level.

"You think you are smart. You think you know everything, but you are just a child. A boy. You know nothing compared to a doctor. You stay away from my daughter and you do as you are told."

"Do you even know why people are sick? I'm quite certain your daughter does."

"They are sick because of a common cold! Contracted by those filthy animals!" Nan Ji roared, pointing a long-nailed finger at the maramuti. "The terrible hygiene on this ship and letting those foul beasts run wild has contaminated everything!"

Wolflock raised an eyebrow, and he swore his maramuti friend did too.

"If you want to help, you will do as your told and nothing more. Do not think you are more clever than Gege. His intelligence will have your mind in spirals."

Wolflock could only shake his head as Nan Ji stalked away, but his maramuti friend felt the need to express his displeasure by throwing a few brown pellets at Nan Ji's back. The shot was good and Wolflock raced downstairs, laughing, before he could get into any trouble.

As he entered the cabin hallway, he could smell fried tuiti fruit and realised that Goden must have served morning tea in everyone's rooms. Mothy was still fast asleep in his militantly neat bed. Wolflock retreated into his own room and he helped his maramuti friend escape out the window.

Nü appeared at his door only moments later.

"I am sorry for my father..."

"He's as charming as the vampires I knew back in Plugh. Perhaps a little less."

Nü sighed and approached as he picked up his plate of tuiti fruit slices, his stomach lurching away from them instinctually.

"Do you really think it's a common cold?"

"If father says it is..." she shrugged and looked out of the window.

She doesn't.

Wolflock didn't much like her just standing in his room, so he moved to the window and flicked the tuiti fruit slices out.

"Oh no... whoops," he drawled with a smirk. "I guess no tuiti fruit for me. What a shame."

She took a step back and her dark almond eyes grew wide. It was unnerving to see the whites all the way around them.

"Are... Nü, are you well?"

She shook her head, nodded and then ran out of the room in a flash, leaving Wolflock perplexed. His maramuti friend poked his head back in through the window, apparently sharing his sentiment.

"What a strange girl."

Wolflock looked into the river out of the window,

scratching the maramuti's head.

"Well, Houl. I hope you're better at hiding things than anyone else on this ship. Otherwise this is going to be the easiest puzzle yet."

CHAPTER 5

Friendly Foes

L unch hadn't yet been served when Wolflock heard Yifi telling Veluse that Tinni, Faleen and Bleen had each fallen ill. All of them displayed the same symptoms. Stomach cramps and watery, clear vomit, the same as Grogen. Wolflock found Gege and told him he'd been given permission to help them carry their herbs up to the kitchen and transform it into a dispensary. The slender boy looked as if he would cry with relief.

Wolflock followed him into the hull, eyed off by Goden as they passed, and showed him the bags and jars that needed to be brought upstairs.

Wolflock instantly regretted his decision to help.

There were over thirty various herbs, minerals and dried animal pieces that needed to be brought up, and all of them were so big that it would take an individual trip to transport them.

"Why does your father need so many herbs?"

Gege scratched his head, pulling some of his long black hair from its braid. "He wanted to show the people of Grothener, Quarenth and Shiriling what our herbal formulas could do so they would want to buy from our clinic back in Xiayah."

"You're over halfway through your journey if that's right. How many did you start with? It must have been an astronomical amount!"

Gege let out a choking laugh. "I cannot remember. I remember we had a few caravan's full."

"Twelve," Nü spoke softly from behind them. "I remember the camels as we crossed Uluken to the Saving River. Father was quite cross that they spit."

Gege laughed and picked up one of the smaller bags. "That is right! Didi got in trouble for laughing."

The two black haired children laughed like tinkling chimes, with the occasional snort from Gege, as they ascended the stairs again. Nü stopped two thirds of the way up the stairs and looked at Wolflock with a blank stare.

"Will you take a box and bring it?" she asked with an air of suspicion. Wolflock was intrigued at how subtle her expressions were. It was as if she was a life-sized porcelain doll with only the slightest enchantment laid across it.

"I'm going to organise them, so they're taken up at the most efficient pace and positioned more effectively when they are in the kitchen."

"How will you know which herbs are used more than others and should be at the front?"

Wolflock blinked.

Nü had questioned him. Not only had she questioned him, but she'd called out his bluff. He felt a pit of indignation settle in his stomach like a hot coal.

"The wear on the bags and oil from hands on the boxes tells me everything I need to know about which ones are more used. In addition, I shall clarify with your father and brother about the correct positioning as we progress, since they are meant to be the medical genii aboard."

Check.

He knew that Nü was smarter than she appeared. Far brighter than Gege, but she had played the part of humble servant to her father and brother, so she would either have to admit she was more educated and more in control than she had lead anyone to believe or she would have to leave Wolflock to his 'organization'.

Her eyes narrowed and her mouth twitched, but she said nothing and retreated upstairs.

Checkmate.

Wolflock knew she would return quickly to observe him again, so he had only moments to search the hull for anywhere a body could have been stored, recently dead animals, whatever booze there was, the non-degradable waste storage and the tank Geagle had mentioned that stored befouled waste. He was beginning to grow suspicious of her odd behaviour. The fear in her eyes when he'd thrown out his food, her medical knowledge when she was not meant to be a physician and her suspicious watchfulness made him wonder if she knew things he didn't. The tank was the easiest to find. It was built into the bottom of the ship and created the flat floor. There was a sealed funnel that lead into it and only when he drew close could he tell it hadn't been opened for quite some time. It was dry, scentless and the latch was flaked with rust.

They'll be bringing down the first full buckets after lunch most likely. Thankfully it has only been coming out of their top ends. There's also the fact that no one was sick with something odd prior to the illness infecting the ship.

The thread resulting in the ship being cursed from Houl due to diseased befoulment being thrown into his river slipped out of his web of clues and dispersed. He sighed, satisfied with his deductions and turned around to search for more evidence. He'd been convinced all along that Houl's curse was fictitious, but now he was more sure than ever. Just beyond the funnel was a sort of penned off area containing some broken plates, wood chips, glass shards and torn bags. Wolflock frowned at it.

Is this all the non-degradable waste the ship produces? Broken bits and pieces? But the more he thought about it the more likely it seemed. The crew maintained every piece of the ship with extreme care and fastidiousness. If anything was broken it was mended and, if it couldn't be mended, it was repurposed. Only after it was deemed completely useless was it taken away. Anything wooden was used in the stove fire. He couldn't help but feel a swell of admiration for the ship and how effectively it functioned.

Wolflock scanned the rest of the dark room with his crystal blue eyes. It was dimly lit by fairy dust lanterns, but he could see the general shapes and locations of what was stored.

Each passenger had an allotment directly under their rooms, interspaced with crates and barrels for the day to day needs of the ship. He was quite impressed with the layout now that it looked at it properly. Empty barrels, crates and sacks were placed on the edges (The one he and Mothy had hid in was positioned at the rear) and there was an inner walkway that allowed access to everything with ease. Most of the passengers only had small amounts of luggage kept in their space, such as trunks and suitcases too small to hold a body. Some had rolls of fabric or furniture wrapped in cloth, while others had more specific items like canvases, belted book stacks or children's dollhouses. Nothing big enough to house a body. The only containers large enough for that were the ship's barrels and crates. He could smell no death or decay, though, and he knew that kind of smell was very hard to hide.

I just need to ask the crew who have been posted at the crow's nest for the last three days if they've seen anyone dumping anything, and the improper disposal of a body line of thought will be eliminated.

He couldn't smell any dead animals either. He weaved as quickly as he could through the luggage but found nothing. The most he found was a crate of salted dried meat, but that was it. He knew that although the hull was clear, he would have to check the deck and perhaps the passengers' rooms to confirm this theory too, but the likelihood of finding a deceased creature was limited to maramuti and birds. He doubted anyone on board besides Mothy was fast enough to catch a bird and no one seemed to dislike the maramuti... except Nan Ji.

Surely not. He's a mean spirited taciturn old man, but not an animal killer.

Wolflock turned to the bags upon bags of herbal medicines and wondered if he had killed something in order to utilise its innards. He began rapidly digging through the bags, sniffing each and reorganising them.

Nothing fresh, at least. Again, he hit another dead end confirming that Houl had not cursed the vessel, but then a dark thought crept into his mind. Did Nan Ji kill and throw a maramuti overboard? Is he trying to heal the sick in order to protect his own wrongdoing? Or did he make people ill in the first place in order to try and advertise his capabilities? How do I find proof if it's true?

Shaking his head, he brought himself back to finish his current investigation. He had to determine one thing at a time, or his evaluations would be skewed by bias.

Now for the...booze? Wolflock realised he didn't know what that word meant. Was it some kind of forbidden dish? Was it a sailor's term for something? He'd have to ask Geagle to give him clearer information.

"Are the herbs organised properly?"

Wolflock jumped with a start, whirling around to see Nü watching him like a viper ready to strike. Her face bore the emotion of a reptile, and yet he felt quite endangered by the young lady.

"Yes. I believe so. They will be transported with ease now."

She looked him up and down, clenching her fists.

"Shall we take some more bags up?" Wolflock cleared his throat and picked up two sacks of grainy herbs.

"No. I will check and make sure they are arranged properly, so they are taken with the most efficient pace up to the kitchen."

Wolflock was taken aback. Was she threatening him? Was she teasing him? He couldn't tell. He just shrugged as nonchalantly as he could and trotted up the stairs.

As he climbed into the midday sunshine, he was nearly knocked down by Geagle as the oaf trampled over him.

"There yah are! I got the log for yah."

Wolflock pressed his now sore toe into his calf to

stem the pain and grimaced as he took the tidy folder, neatly punched with holes and tied with smooth twine so pages could be removed and replaced with ease.

"Thank you," he said with a wince. "How did you obtain this document?"

Geagle thought for a moment. It looked hard.

"I asked Slavidus. He kinda rolled over and showed it to me. Poor man looks bloody awful. And now, just after lunch, Veluse and Froderyk got sick, too. Please find a way to lift the curse before Houl takes another one!"

Wolflock's eyes flashed, "What do you mean 'another'?"

"I-I shouldn'ta said nothin'," he swallowed. "Just that I don't wanna see anyone else get crook is all..."

"Geagle? What do you know?"

"I-It ain't' for me to say. All I know is that last time the ship got this sick, someone died. It's all I know. Goden keeps joking it's gonna be me cause I looked like 'im!"

Wolflock expected to see absolute fear in Geagle at his last words, but there was contempt. He wasn't afraid to get sick. He was afraid of someone else dying. Wolflock thought it might be for his beloved crewmates.

"It'll be fine. I'm well on my way to finding the

source of this issue. Let me look at the cargo log and we'll see if I can confirm something. Take these bags into the kitchen and I'll..."

Wolflock trailed off as Geagle shot off. He flicked open to the most recent entry.

8th of Eolas Revari, 11th Year of King Rayin's rule

Dock: Plugh
Incoming
Cargo Type: Passenger Luggage Payment (Mr Felen)
Quantity: 3, 30 yards
Record of Operations: 2 medium trunks and one satchel to Mr Wolflock F. Felen departing Corsh. 1 trunk stored. Canvas sails rolled and place in section 25.4
Outgoing
Cargo Type: Postal
Quantity: crate of 50
Record of Operations: Parcels and packages from Corl to Plugh as commissioned by Royal Postal Service.

He flipped back to the logs taken at the South Pyringel crossing, Una, Corl, Ropoa, and all the way back to the first log taken at Shellinden.

Medicine, sewing materials, tools, jewellery, books, pots, and animal supplies, but no mention of bodies, or this mysterious "booze". Everything was all ordinary and rather bland. Wolflock concluded that the cargo log simply confirmed his belief that no one had the means to bring a body on board, let alone dispose of it this far up river.

Good. That clears up another trail. There is no chance someone could have killed an animal and hidden it on the ship without the stench being noticed. Another trail cleared up. Now I only have to ask the crew on crow's nest duty for the last three or four days and this foolish curse of Houl hypothesis is eliminated.

"Ahem."

Wolflock closed the folder with a 'thump' and looked up to see Nü scowling at him.

"Can I help you?" he raised an eyebrow.

"I thought you were trying to help Mr Enitel... Enitvela..."

"Enitnelav. His name is Mothy Enitnelav."

Nü raised her nose. "Your assistance is needed in the kitchen. Father wants you to clean the-"

"You know what, Miss Nü Nan? I believe my services are more effective elsewhere. I'll be doing my own searching for the source of this illness. I'm sure your family is more than capable of helping aid the symptoms of our fellow shipmates."

Wolflock smirked as he watched the quiet girl's face burn crimson across her cheeks.

"He is-it is-" she opened her mouth to tell him off but bit back her words, her shaking fists gripping her dress tightly. "My medicine treats the root cause of sickness. It does not merely treat symptoms."

"*'My medicine*?'" Wolflock parroted with a derisive snort.

"I meant to say my *family's* medicine."

"Miss Nan?" Captain Blutro appeared at Wolflock's side and pointedly removed the cargo log from his hands. "I hope our young friend here isn't bothering you, is he?"

Although he stood as firmly as ever, Wolflock couldn't help but notice dark bags under the Captain's eyes. With every breath his face twitched in pain and his left hand sat just a little too high on his hip, putting pressure on his abdomen.

"I was just asking Mr Wolflock for assistance in the kitchen," Nü dropped her gaze.

"Very good. The Nan family needs all hands until dinner. Good lad for volunteering."

"I did not volunteer."

"Very well," Captain Blutro nodded with an air of deep understanding. "I, as captain of this vessel hereby charge you with the transference of duties. Since your writing duties cannot be fulfilled at this time due to the incapacitation of the crew, you shall be indentured to the Nan family's wishes until such time as I deem your retribution paid, or until the week is up."

Wolflock snarled. "That wasn't our agreement! I won't do it. I am a paying customer and you shall not hold me to these fickle rules!"

"Miss Nan, will you give us a moment?"

Nü nodded and stood by the dining hall entrance in an attempt to be surreptitious.

"You were content to help earlier, I was told. What difference does it make that you're held to your word?"

"I *offered* to help before. I volunteered my time and efforts. I have recently found more effective employment and wanted to retract my offer."

Blutro sighed, "So it has to be on your terms and to keep you entertained, does it, Master Felen?"

"Ideally," Wolflock looked down his long nose as he picked at his nails.

"I give you an inch and you think you deserve the whole river. Fine. I would like you to volunteer to serve in the employ of the crew and Nan family until this sickness is cured."

Wolflock was about to retort sardonically, but the weak, pasty face of the recently powerful Captain quelled his pride. It was the exact same exhausted look his father had given him the week his mother had been taken.

"Aye, aye, Captain."

Captain Blutro clapped Wolflock on the back and looked back towards the cabin.

"I'll discover the cause of the sickness."

Wolflock strode towards the dining hall as Captain Blutro tried to call after him, "That's not what I ordered you to do" before a coughing fit took him.

He began to shuffle away when Wolflock saw him stop and lean heavily on the mast, clutching his stomach.

If Captain falls ill the ship will stop sailing again, just like what nearly happened when his snuffle was missing.

He turned back to Nü, who was also watching after Captain Blutro.

"Very well. But I'm only helping until dinner. Then I'm conducting my own investigation."

Nü's shoulders relaxed, "Come inside. You must clean the cups and collect herbs when father demands it."

"Marvellous. Exactly how I wanted to spend my afternoon."

There was something to be said for a monotonous task like washing dishes or serving food. It took so little brainpower and became such a mere muscle memory chore that Wolflock felt as if he were able to hone in all of his mental power, undistracted by his other occupied senses.

Slavidus and Captain Blutro take turns to do admin work and drive the ship, occasionally swapping with Canhop, who is second mate, when the new fortnightly roster has to be developed. Then there are the engineers. An ebony gentleman from Syongdelen and the tall, chestnut woman who may be from the border of Syongdelen and Quarenth, who takes care of the machinery and working parts of the ship on alternate day and night shifts. The rest of the seven remaining crew rotate between deck duties, cooking, entertaining and crow's nest duties, but whoever is on night watch is off duty during the day. Goden and Hognut have been cooks for the last two days and that should rotate back to Groger and Matroos, with the goose tattoo, which means that Kolor, Geagle, Goden and Groger were in the crow's nest over the last three or four days. I can ask them if anyone has dumped anything overboard. Then, I can start looking into what is actually causing this illness. Is it the maramuti? They're not trying to get into the kitchen at the moment. Is it the smell of the medicine? What if it's the food that's been cooked improperly?

A dark voice whispered in the back of his mind as he pressed his leg into the cupboard door, feeling the lump of strange handkerchief in his pocket.

Is someone making the crew and company ill for another purpose? But why? What could it be? Everyone on the ship appears ultimately harmless...

"These are all wrong! We needed the ingredients for my modification of Gé Gēn Tāng, not Shēng Má Gégēn Tāng! Who brought up these herbs?" Nan Ji roared as he held the label on the jar inches from his face.

He can't see well...

"Sorry, father," Gege winced. "I will go get the-"

"I will go! If you want something done right, you have to do it yourself!" Nan Ji stormed out, banging the doors savagely.

A heavy silence fell across the room with only the bubbling cauldron of medicine and the occasional bump of cups on benches. The three children all looked very tense, even the youngest, Didi.

"Is he always like that?"

None of them even met his eye. They didn't trust him. Wolflock sniffed and thought of what Mothy might do to earn their trust.

'*People like it when you ask them questions,*' echoed in his mind.

"My father gets like that sometimes. Are you all training to be physicians?"

"Yes..." the youngest heaved a glum sigh.

Gege nodded and glanced up at Nü as if asking for permission.

"But your father won't let you touch the herbs. How can you learn?" Wolflock asked pointedly at her. He knew she wasn't being trained, but he wanted to find out why. He suspected feigning ignorance would help him pry for answers.

Nü's jaw tensed.

"I'm not training to become a physician."

"What? Why? Aren't your whole family doctors? Don't tell me everyone in Xiayah hates women like your father-"

"Mr Wolflock, please understand!" Gege pleaded, "Our mother was a doctor. Her and father ran a clinic together, but she was made very sick by one of her patients. Women are just not strong enough to fend off disease. Father won't permit Nü to study with us because he treasures her-"

Gege stopped as Nü turned and walked away from them.

Again, the door banged shut and again the heavy silence fell upon them.

"She wants to learn, doesn't she?" Wolflock asked, his voice filled with pity.

"More than anything..." Gege sighed. "She was raised learning about herbs more than playing games with other girls. Then, when mother passed away, father stopped her from doing any of it."

"He just took it all away from her? Like that?"

Gege nodded as he hung his head as he counted out some dried berries.

"Please do not tell her I said anything, Mr Wolflock. It is hard enough for her not even being allowed to touch the herbs, let alone learn about them."

The poor boy looked so tired. Bags hung under his dropping almond eyes and his cheeks looked like wet paper. Wolflock could only nod. When he had first seen the Nan family he had thought they looked prim, proper, and well educated. Now he realised that were just like any other professional family. Filled with politics, hierarchy and strange rules that would never be applied in average families.

They'd fit in well in Plugh...

Nan Ji returned sometime after and argued with Goden about how much space he needed in the kitchen.

Wolflock and the two Nan boys took this as a good enough chance to deem the medicine sufficiently prepared and had just enough time to put it into cups before Goden threw a Tuiti fruit at them.

He's covering for Groger on cooking duties... he must be exhausted. Wolflock narrowed his eyes and surveyed the situation.

Goden was beginning to look pale too, but he was still robust as ever. He thought he may as well try his luck as they made it to the door.

"Haven't seen anyone dumping things over the ship on your watch have you, Goden?"

"I'll dump you over the ship if you don't skedaddle outta my kitchen!" he thundered and threw another tuiti fruit. Closing the door to shield himself, Wolflock heard a satisfying squelch from the other side.

"I'll take that as a no." Wolflock chuckled as he watched the fruit slide down the glass pane in the door.

The three boys took the cups of acrid smelling medicine to the sick passengers. Wolflock offered to bring them to the sick crewmates. There were more than before. Grogen was on the only one to sit up at the sight of him. None of them were in their hammocks.

"Ah, Wolflock. Good lad. Is that Nan Ji's mix?"

"Yes, Grogen. Here. Hopefully, it will make you

feel a bit better."

"'Sgotta be better than Geagle makin' out we're dyin' every half hour. Poor lad's never really seen a ship get ill this fast. S'alright though. Ship folk get better faster than land folk."

"If you say so."

"S'nice to 'ave a day to rest though," Grogen mumbled to himself after he drank down the draught entirely.

Wolflock could only smile at the mountain of a man snuggling down into his bedding like a giant, bearded baby. It was certainly a sight he thought he'd never see. Wolflock was able to question Kolor and Groger at the same time as they were both feeling ill. He fed them their medicine and found out that neither of them had witnessed anything out of the ordinary in regards to passenger behaviour.

Houl did not curse this ship. Wolflock concluded and with satisfaction, removed his thread of reasoning from the case's web. He would report it to Geagle when he next saw him. That only left a few theories to explore.

Had the food been cooked improperly? Were the maramuti diseased? Or had someone intentionally made the ship's crew and company ill?

The easiest one to rule out was if the food had

been improperly cooked. Knowing Goden was in a foul temper this evening, he had to tread lightly, but Wolflock had an idea of how to get around the Corshman's bad mood.

He re-entered the dining hall, seeing Stra, Yifi and Fuhji playing cards, and slunk along the edges, hoping not the catch Goden's eye just yet. The saccharine stench of tuiti fruit soup and dried ginger made him want to gag, but he persisted.

"So... Goden," he said in a soothing, gentle tone, "Would you like a hand with dinner?"

He could see it was nearly finished, so at most he'd be asked to serve the plates.

Goden raised a bushy eyebrow. "Nah, lad. Yeh can take the plates if yeh want. Most people in bed this evening. Captain says if Nan Ji's potion works good, we'll have a second dinner to celebrate. Good ol' Nan Ji thinks it'll work in an hour or so."

"That soon?"

"Oh, aye. Should be all fine soon."

"That's good. I wanted to ask... you're the best cook on the ship, how do you prepare the tuiti fruit? It smells," he swallowed, "delicious."

Goden puffed out his chest with pride. "Good ta see someone knows cul-loon-in-ary brilliance when they look at it. C'mon round and I'll show yeh."

Wolflock chuckled to himself. It was always so easy to get the crew to do what he wanted. A bit of flattery and they were like putty in his hand.

"Now, first things first-"

"Pick up the knife and cut it?"

"No, lad! We ain't savages! Wash yeh hands. Yeh gotta be clean in a kitchen."

Had Wolflock not baited him to do it, he would have been offended by Goden's abrasive discipline. He tried over and over, but Goden kept reciting that the ship was for better calibre people and that he wouldn't tolerate anything less than perfect in his kitchen. Wolflock couldn't tell if he was putting it on because he had an audience, but the rigidity of the hour's training definitely told him that the kitchen would not tolerate any mistakes that lead to food contamination. Again, on a similar level to the amount of waste the ship produced, Wolflock was thoroughly impressed with the training of the crew. With such structure and discipline, he assumed they would have to be cold, cut throat and inhospitable, but the crew were always jovial and made a game out of their work while sticking to the tight rules that had been placed on them. It just deepened his appreciation for the entire Silver Ice Hair.

But it didn't prove his hypothesis.

He glared out of Goden's line of sight at the bubbling stew. The fluorescent pink and green colours were thinning into a grey mush, with the larger chunks bobbing on the surface menacingly. The food, although insufferably sweet, was not the likely cause of the illness.

He was back to square one. His web of clues had no leads. Now it was merely the maramuti bringing disease on the ship or something more sinister.

He finished his lesson with Goden, dizzy from the thick smell of Tuiti fruit. Wolflock took a large jug of water from the kitchen and found immense comfort hanging halfway over the port side taffrail in the cool Autumn air. After a moment he just poured the jug over his head, letting it wash down his face. His black hair covered his closed eyes and he blew an undignified raspberry through the torrent of water. The thick stench of Tuiti fruit and Xiayahn herbs lingered, but at least it had been rinsed off enough that he no longer wanted to gag. The cool water was so refreshing and seemed to rejog his brain, but he wanted to bounce his ideas off something or someone. Before he left Plugh, he would do this with Myna or his horse Brennan, but, while he was on the ship, he had an abundance of people who may be able to give insight into a variety of topics, all of which were in poor health currently.

He felt something by his elbow and reached down for the jug along his arm. An adolescent maramuti was trying to get to his jug. He noted that they had quite shiny fur as they got older. Their huge round eyes didn't move much, but their heads turned further than a person's could. Their little claws and round tipped digits looked like an otter's and the males tails were long and slender with a flat broad disc at the end, whereas the females have a flat baton shaped one. There didn't appear to be any mange, they didn't sneeze or cough, and he certainly hadn't seen them vomit or display any signs of gut disturbances.

"Do you feel ill?" Wolflock asked the creature. It just looked back at him before persisting with the jug. "I'll take that as a no."

The friendly little creature touched the jug, putting its whole head inside as Wolflock ran his hand over its thick fur.

"No fleas or lice?" he leaned in a little closer behind it as the maramuti held the jug in both hands, biting the rim. "You smell odd... not like an animal."

The maramuti smelt acrid, but also a little minty. There were no fleas or lice on the creature, but there were flecks of yellow pollen and two very distinct types of freshly crushed leaves through its fur.

They must roll in it or something. It's as strong as citronella, but it's a different herb. At least it's not Tuiti fruit. Mothy likes herbs. He may be able to tell me what it is... I wonder if he's awake...

Wolflock petted the maramuti, wiping the herbs onto his handkerchief and plucking a few of the longer strands from its back. He returned briefly to the kitchen to get a tray of tea, tuiti fruit and bread, before heading down to see if Mothy was awake. As he carefully descended the stairs, he could hear Mothy's voice in the midst of a story. He could hear the smile on his friend's face.

"... and then he said 'you were supposed to treat my mother-in-law! Not my cow!', and the doctor replied, 'I thought I *did* treat her!'"

Mothy laughed at his own joke, but it surprised Wolflock to hear Nü's tinkling laugh follow. He knocked on the doorframe with his foot and maneuvered the tray into the room. Nü was sitting a little too casually on the edge of Mothy's dishevelled bed, her dainty form more relaxed than Wolflock had ever seen her.

"Evening, Invalid. You're looking better"

"Evening, Lockie," Mothy grinned from ear to ear. "Yum! Second dinner!"

Wolflock passed him the tray of Tuiti fruit stew and snatched up the hempseed bread, leaning on the desk in the room.

"Come now," Nü protested with a playful tone, setting her hand on the tray across Mothy's lap. "Have not you had enough dinner?"

"You can never have enough food. Food is love!" Mothy scoffed three mouthfuls before he finished his sentence, but, as he did, both he and Nü blushed furiously.

"I... I should see if father needs help. If you need me, I am only a few rooms away." Her voice was soft and tender, as it was with all her patients, but Wolflock couldn't help but notice she smiled more at Mothy. She slipped out of the room but lingered at the door frame before she disappeared.

Mothy's hand had reached out to catch her, but he'd missed. His whole body slumped in smitten relief and his soft blue eyes lingered over where she had been.

Wolflock coughed. "Who knew you only had to become deathly ill, and you'd have the attention of the girl you're infatuated with."

Mothy coughed and polished off the rest of the stew in a few gulps. After a few moments his face had gone from beetroot red to pink again.

"In your words: I'm sure I don't know what you mean."

Wolflock raised an eyebrow, smirking.

"Alright, alright. I was very pleased to spend the last few hours with her. She's so..." Mothy trailed off.

"Pretty?" Wolflock wanted to add 'suspicious', but he didn't want to spoil his friend's good mood.

"Kind," Mothy corrected him. "She sat with me all afternoon to make sure I was alright because she knew you were busy in the kitchen. She even made me this delicious dinner of jerky, jam and dried vegetables. Not too filling, but it's the thought that counts."

Jerky? Wolflock's mind snapped to attention. "What kind of jerky?"

"Not sure. She said it was something from Xiayah. I'll ask her when she gives me my next medicine. I'm feeling so much better."

"I'm glad to hear it. I think everyone is starting to recover. Nan Ji must actually know what he's doing."

"I sure hope so."

"Speaking of 'knowing what you're doing', I found these leaves on a maramuti. Do you know what they are?" Wolflock pulled out his handkerchief and unwrapped the herbs he'd collected.

Mothy looked at them carefully, pinched them, sniffed them and touched them with the tip of his tongue.

"Well, this one is tansy. It's got that acrid smell and the yellow bits are from the flowers. I know this smell anywhere. We used to use it to keep bugs away in Summer... and Spring... and Autumn. Chalongesh. You get flies all year round. This other one, though... It's minty but not. Maybe ask Nü. She'll know."

Wolflock nodded and wrapped them back up in his handkerchief.

"Goden said we might be having a second dinner tonight to celebrate everyone getting better. Nan Ji was very confident in his abilities. We can ask Nü about the plant together. Want to come up for dinner number three?"

"Do I?" Mothy threw off his blankets and began pulling on his jacket.

Wolflock stood aside and saw that he started belching and then he clutched his stomach in pain.

"Actually... Maybe I shouldn't. I mustn't be fully recovered yet. Bring me some down will... will you?"

Mothy trailed off, starting to sweat heavily as he sat back down.

"You're going pale. Here. Drink my tea. Get your jacket off and lay back down," Wolflock commanded.

"Aye... aye... Take my dishes up please, Lockie? I don't want them to attract bugs or maramuti. They keep... trying to steal my... hairbrush..."

Within moments of his friend nestling back under his covers, his eyes were closed. It was such an alarming change that Wolflock grew very concerned.

What if Nü hasn't been giving him the same formula as everyone else? What if she has modified it? I have to speak to her. What if she's making him more ill?

As he took the tray back to the dining hall, he started to think of when the illness started. Nü had come out with tea for her family, meaning she had been one of the last people to go to the kitchen before the illness struck. She was very defensive of the herbs and he had seen her hiding something when he'd collected buckets for her. His suspicion mounting, Wolflock entered the dining hall and spotted Nü being thanked by Dlumi and Haatji. He gave the dishes back to Goden before questioning her so he could get the answers he needed without her running off. Stra, the botanist, was preparing his own meal at the bench and sprinkling pinches of herbs on a cut of meat.

"Merry meet, Stra. Have you been well?"

"Better than most," the sharp-faced man replied dryly.

"Looks like everyone is better now though. I was starting to think the food had been poisoned or something like that. Thankfully, the Nan family came to the ship's aid." Even as he spoke, the words felt wrong. He hadn't discovered the cause of the illness. What was stopping it from striking again?

"Mmm... Not possible. Poison would have made the food very bitter and someone would have noticed it." Stra uncorked a vile of purplish powder and sprinkled it thoroughly over the meat, massaging it in before putting it on a sizzling hot frying pan.

"You're a herbalist, yes?"

"Botanist." Stra looked flatly down his nose.

"An educated man at least. Have you any thoughts on what brought this disease to the ship?"

"I can only hazard a guess. What were your theories?"

"You would know better than I, I'm sure. I ruled out the maramuti bringing disease onto the ship and I determined that the cooking processes in the kitchen were better than most manor houses, so contamination isn't the issue. It's certainly not this 'curse of Houl' theory Geagle had. The only thought I had was that someone had deliberately made people sick, but I couldn't think of a means of delivery. The ship displayed signs of illness before Nan Ji had treated them so it couldn't be him..."

Stra eyed him suspiciously. "I wouldn't go blaming anyone for this illness. What could anyone possibly gain from making the people here sick? Prestige? Unlikely. I'd say it was merely an accident. There is so much that goes on around here, we can't expect the crew to see everything at all times. I'd say it was simply some off food."

"Interesting hypothesis..." Wolflock's face clearly displayed his dissatisfaction with the answer. "When I get to Mystentine, I'll be studying these things intensely, though. Perhaps our paths will cross again, and you can test my knowledge."

Stra served himself the rare steak, still bleeding onto the plate, as he stepped away from the conversation.

"I'm sure we shall, Lockie."

Wolflock nodded in response and looked around for Nü. The women she'd been talking to had taken their seats and were eating more tuiti fruit stew. Wolflock took a new loaf of bread from the bag and made his way towards her. As he did, he heard Froderyk let out a loud belch, causing most of the table to laugh. In response, Veluse released a rather deep belch, followed by Tinni, who let out the deepest of them all.

With an amused snort, Wolflock took his herb

buttered bread and sat by Nü. Her head was bowed like usual, but she was gripping her skirt so hard it looked like it would rip.

"Merry meet, Nü. Are you well?" Wolflock whispered as Captain Blutro began announcing his joy at seeing everyone well and bright again. "I wanted to ask you about this herb-"

He was cut off by Dlumi letting out the daintiest burp he could have ever fathomed and causing the table to explode into raucous laughter. Everyone laughed so hard they gripped their stomachs and began sweating.

She looked up at him, the whites of her eyes glaring through the curtain of black hair. Her eyes flicked over the little string of leaves he presented. She snatched it and sniffed it, then dropped it back in his hands.

"Do you have fleas?" she seemed to accuse, her eyes darting around at anyone else who belched loudly.

"What? No! I found it on a maramuti."

"It is pennyroyal. It repels fleas and many insects."

"So, the maramuti are relatively clean... interesting. Whatever has got you so agitated?"

"It is not right."

"What's not right?"

"*They* are not right."

Bowls of empty stew filled the table, the pungent

sweetness thick in the air.

Captain Blutro's broad smile faltered as the crew and company, who were buckled over with laughter, began groaning in pain. His skin went pale and the sweat on his forehead dripped down his strong jaw. With a disgusting splash, the captain had emptied the contents of his stomach on the floor in front of him, his toasting goblet clattering to the rug.

Half the table gasped while the other began throwing up their dinner too. Nü pushed her chair back in horror and Wolflock jumped to his feet.

Captain Blutro had begun vomiting blood.

The dining hall door banged open and as Wolflock whirled around he saw Faleen holding her twin Bleen, soaked from the rain and blood trickling from their mouths.

"It's the curse of Houl!" she sobbed. "He's going to kill us all!"

Rhiannon D. Elton

CHAPTER 6
The Sick Sinking Ship

The heavy chinking, scraping noise of the anchor being dropped into the water, and the heart sinking splash it caused nearly made Wolflock sick. Second mate Canhop, a dark-haired gentleman with olive skin and a passion for maps, decreed that during the evenings the ship would drop anchor as there just weren't enough crew to man the ship day and night.

Wolflock felt more trapped now than he had ever felt in his life. He would surely miss the deadline to enroll at Mystentine if they travelled at this pace. The pit in his stomach flung terrible thoughts into his mind of having to drag his bags back home through Plugh with those wretched stares. The whole town would line up to gawk at his failure. They'd point and whisper, and he would be without any support. Any friend at all. Even Myna would be forced to follow suit in order to maintain her own reputation.

As the dark water washed over the chain links of the anchor, Wolflock felt as if his fate was chained to that same darkness. There was only one time in his life that he felt more helpless. He couldn't bear to think about that, though, so he drew his thoughts back to the explosion of chaos that ensued only an hour or so beforehand.

The dining hall had grown so quiet that only the waves of rain could be heard. Hognut had been the first to break the silence.

"Don't be a fool, yah silly witch."

Nan Ji had rushed to the Captain's side and Slavidus had tried to aid him even though he was covered in his own vomit as well.

"We've been cursed for travelling across Houl's sacred waters!" Faleen wailed as Bleen hung limply in her sister's arms. "He's angry that we didn't pay any tribute! Our cards have spoken!"

"But why? He didn't ask for tribute! There were

no signs! Why would he make us suffer?" Veluse pleaded, throwing himself at Faleen's feet and tearing at her dress, tears streaking down his ghostly face.

"Don't indulge them, yah daffy fool!" Hognut growled.

"Hognut! Goden! Get them all to bed. Nan Ji, please get your family to do something!" Canhop spoke loudly, but his voice trembled and his whole body shook like a leaf.

"It's the curse!" Geagle shrieked, before he caught Parihaan as she fell into convulsions. "They're right!"

Wolflock had had enough. He turned to leave and saw that Nü had already disappeared. His head ached from it all. Nothing made sense. His web had fallen apart.

No one had warranted the wrath of Houl. The maramuti had not brought disease to the ship. The crew had cooked the food to the highest standard. Even this proved that Nan Ji had not intentionally made people ill.

Nan Ji would only be praised for making people well again and "saving" the ship. There had been a motive. He was travelling in order to build prestige for his medical prowess. He'd been an absolute horror to work with and appeared blundering to Wolflock when it came to his own medicine, and he'd also been in charge of distributing medicine to all those who were ill, but there were two key pieces of evidence that showed he was not the culprit. Firstly, he had no original opportunity to initiate the illness. Secondly, had he actually poisoned the ship, then he would not have chosen to have them all relapse during the moment he was getting recognised for his medical prowess.

It would either have been a very poorly executed plot, or, as Wolflock now suspected, there was no plot at all.

But if there was no plot... Wolflock shook his head as he stood up straight. Something wasn't right. Now that every thread of thought had been plucked out of his web, he felt like he was grasping at straws. As his frustration began to boil in his stomach, it drove out his wretched self-pity. Everyone had been taken to their cabins and the Nan family had continued their revolving buckets and concoctions. Wolflock had been ordered to help, but he had stopped to collect his thoughts as the anchor was lowered.

What is the source of the illness? Geagle said this has happened before. I need more data! He pinched the bridge of his long nose and closed his eyes. A flash of recollection burst into his mind.

The Captain has logs! He will have something to shed light on this!

"Whatcha doin', lad?" grumbled a sour faced Goden.

"Watching my dreams sink to the bottom of the river..." Wolflock sighed, reshuffling the buckets to refill them.

"Ain't no time for that. C'mon. You and me is on cleaning duty."

Wolflock made a face. More chores.

"For how long?"

"Til it's done. Now, hop to."

Wolflock didn't protest beyond making some faces and huffing sighs. There were only three remaining able-bodied crew. They needed all hands-on deck. And Wolflock needed a way to find more data. Having access to the entire ship through the means of aiding the Nan family would let him get to where he needed to search without trouble.

For the rest of the evening, Wolflock worked by lantern-light alongside Hognut, Goden and Canhop. They used a solution of soapwort and clove oil to scrub down every single surface the crew and company had been able to touch. Walls, floors, countertops, seats, chairs, door handles, even the tops of the barrels.

At one stage, Canhop asked Nan Ji if he needed any assistance, but the cranky old man just mumbled to himself. "I know what they need. I know what they need," as he stirred his new cinnamon and liquorice tasting concoction. After they purified the ship, Canhop sent Wolflock to bed and told he'd be woken when he was needed. He was so exhausted he fell asleep the instant he hit the pillow, barely aware of the groans and vomiting noises that permeated the night.

The next morning, instead of breakfast, Goden gave Wolflock a tray of six cups, steaming their powerful odours around his face as he made his way back to the cabins. Nü was standing on a chair, hanging up strings of dry herbs over the rooms.

"What are those for?" he asked as he began setting the new healing potions down on the bedside tables of the sick.

"They are to help ward off evil," she said with an expressionless face.

In each room she had hung herbs above, Wolflock found a second cup in each of their rooms.

What is she doing? Did she get them a second dose? Has she been changing the formulas?

"What are the herbs on the doors really for?" Wolflock asked before he entered Mothy's room.

Nü smiled sheepishly. "They are good for digestion. They help to stop vomiting."

"Did you father say to do this?"

She didn't meet his eye. "My father is very busy. This is something small, so I know can help."

As he took the medicine in to Mothy, he couldn't help but wonder if the herbs really did stop vomiting and if Nü was up to much more than her father would permit. His face felt hot, and he tossed his head from side to side restlessly, but the rest of his body stayed as still as a stone.

"Do you know anything about the river god Houl?" Wolflock asked.

"Not very much at all. The river gods in Xiayah are said to be ancient dragons that keep the water flowing. They do not bring illness."

"I lived in Plugh, which is inland from the river, so we didn't learn much about him either. You don't believe it's a curse though, do you?"

Nü's face went blank. "Father believes it is rebellicus stomach qi caused by damp cold."

"That's not what you believe though, is it?"

She looked at him sideways and quickly packed up her things. "I do not understand."

Wolflock eyed her as she left. She'd changed her hair... it was braided, not bundled with her hairpin. He continued giving everyone their medicine until he reached the Captain's room. His work had paid off.

The captain laid in his bed pale and sweating, but it was the rest of the room that bothered Wolflock. He knew Captain Blutro was a militantly tidy man, yet his room was in disarray. Books and papers were scattered everywhere, all with varying images of dark whirlpools, sickness, death and giant creatures crushing ships.

Captain said he didn't believe in the curse... Did he lie?

Wolflock's gut trembled. He had easily dismissed Houl's curse. He had been shown, to his satisfaction, that all of Geagle's parameters hadn't been broken. Why was the captain researching this then?

Wolflock began digging through the notes, filing them away and closing the books he had no use for. He refused to believe that the thread he had ruled out was to be brought back into his web of thoughts. Scrolls, notebooks, journals, maps, charts and other scraps of paper scattered around the room detailed all manner of trivia about the ship and the river. Wolflock scanned each of them and put them away. The room was as tidy as normal and, yet, none of the passing notes or pages in the books had seemed relevant. Aujin, the silver snuffle, circled up his trousers and nestled into his neck as he continued looking.

"Getting enough food, Aujin?" He scratched the

soft silky strands of hair, opening the draws and cabinets to find any other notes.

Aujin let out that odd grunt he had learned that sounded eerily like 'friend', before slithering back down and wriggling under the captain's pillow. Wolflock looked everywhere. The captain's foot chest was locked, as was his safe, but nowhere could Wolflock find the logs that Geagle had mentioned. Apparently, the Silver Ice Hair had always been lucky in its travels. Most of the logs were about new trade deals and dignitaries who had been transported, as well as problems with crew and onboard politics. Nothing remotely interesting.

Seeing nothing under the captain's bed, Wolflock began to extract himself when he felt a small heavy object bounce off his head and clatter onto the floor.

A key?

He looked up to see Aujin staring down at him with its eyeless face. He reached up and scratched the snuffle's flat chin before he picked up the key. It was large and silver, matching the foot chest lock. Wolflock placed it in, opened the chest, and saw neatly stacked books, scrolls, papers and a few odd trinkets. He read through very old festive recipes, charms and enchantments to protect the ship from bad weather, and novels about a family of wandering fools called the Everbottoms.

Wolflock only stopped for a moment to pocket a note about the problems of excessive tuiti fruit consumption so he could give it to Goden later.

Finally, he came across an old blue leather worn book with dark yellow pages and the smell of mildew. The first page was of an artwork of the Silver River from the Silver Lake to Shellinden, but the second page proved far more enlightening.

Captain Beleur Silk's Log,

In the fourteenth year of the reign of Queen Renviri the Generous, on the fourteenth day of the month Ha'ling Felst, between the mountains after the Blickland forest wharf, we have swapped shiny titbits for barrels upon barrels of Tuiti fruit, which has proved most beneficial as the passenger, Forlosk Forchan, did not arrive at Corl with the supplies promised for the journey....

Wolflock's stomach churned harder at the mere word "Tuiti", making him skim ahead to the information he thought was more relevant. Judging by the date and the writer's name, Wolflock deduced it was the captain's grandfather's journal. Apparently, the maramuti had been trading tuiti fruit for generations.

.... In the fourteenth year of the reign of Queen Renviri the Generous, on the sixteenth day of the month Ha'ling Felst, between the mountains of the Dragon's Spine on the Silver River, a brawl broke out between two men. They came aboard together, and it has been discovered that they smuggled drinking alcohol on board and began fighting drunkenly while everyone was on deck for dinner. Feyr came down and found one with his head bashed in with a bottle. We gave him a river burial and tossed all the poison overboard. The second man threw himself off the ship after it. Foolish sod...

.... In the fourteenth year of the reign of Queen Renviri the Generous, on the nineteenth day of the month Ha'ling Felst, just entering the mouth of the Silver Lake, most of our crew and company have fallen deathly ill with vomiting, delirium and sweats. Houl has cursed us thoroughly after the death of the poisoned ones. Only Kaji and Annees are unaffected. We all believe it is due to their spiritual fasting month beginning this moon. They have been blessed by whatever gods they pray to...

... In the fourteenth year of the reign of Queen Renviri the Generous, on the twentieth day of the month Ha'ling Felst, Feyr has died. He began vomiting blood and would not stop. Being such a small lad, it only took a few hours for him to empty himself on the deck and

collapse with no hope of waking him. We buried him at dusk....

... In the fourteenth year of the reign of Queen Renviri the Generous, on the twenty-first day of the month Ha'ling Felst, we finally get reprieve of this forsaken illness. Three more began vomiting blood but no one else passed. It appears Houl has accepted Feyr as his tribute. I had feared we would starve also as we had finally run out of Tuiti fruit and other rations. We found some of the Tuiti fruit were in fact river bug larvae, but as we were so low on rations, we ate them regardless, which was quite unwise because the three that did eat them were the three that began vomiting blood...

"Houl..."

Wolflock thrust the book back into the chest and slammed it shut, clipping his finger. As Wolflock shook his hand furiously and sucked on his blistering finger he saw Captain Blutro lay rigid in his bed. Aujin began 'hroo'ing and slithering back and forth around Blutro's head.

"Captain?" Wolflock approached tentatively, seeing the Captain's dark green eyes staring into nothing.

Unblinking. Unmoving.

He reached out to check the Captain's pulse, but

the man wheezed and grabbed Wolflock's wrist in an iron grip. Wolflock tried to wrench himself free, but the captain was as rigid as the ship's mast.

"Houl... Houl has cursed us..." he wheezed as if he were possessed. "As he did before... he shall do again... seeking vengeance for the lies... the lies of the ship... seeking revenge for the toxins in her belly.... the poison... the poison of his wrath will take our lives..."

As he fainted, Wolflock jerked free and backed up, tripping on the rug and landing hard on his arm. His heart was beating in his ears from the fright and he waited, staring in horror at the softly moaning, restless captain. Aujin continued to purr and "hroo" into Blutro's neck.

Wolflock rubbed his wrist, rising to his feet and backing up to the door.

'In her belly'? Does he mean a woman? Wolflock thought about what possible woman the Captain could be referring to. The most meaningful 'she' Captain appeared to have in his life was the ship. *It must be the hull. Something in the hull must be making people sick still.*

He flew through the door and leaped down the stairs. He had to have missed something. Something reasonable, something explainable, something... something less terrifying. He could handle poison, disease, accidents or even crime. But an unappeasable, non-discriminatory god of a river he wasn't native to? No, sir!

Grabbing a fairy dust lantern and shaking it until it lit up everything around him, Wolflock began hunting. He rechecked everything he had searched before, but the only thing that had changed all that much were that the Nan family's herbs were rearranged. A few sacks of them were even open as if someone had recently been through them.

I brought up all the herbs Nan Ji demanded. Did he change his mind? Did his formula change?

The only other thing he saw was a linen napkin on top of Veluse's box of paints. It was covered with herbs, all neatly separated into little piles. As he held the lantern closer to it, Wolflock saw the same jerky flakes he'd seen outside a few days ago. He took out the handkerchief and compared the two. The jerky amongst the pile of herbs was the same green and pink colours as tuiti fruit... or the river bug larvae. The one in his hand was more purple. Unlike the herbs he'd seen Nan Ji prepare, these ones were also charred. A candle sat snuffed out next to them.

Not a match, but someone has been making up medical potions, and it's not a hard guess as to who.

He moved over to the open bags of herbs and

grinned. Something was glittering inside one, just under a layer of seeds. He pocketed it and felt the satisfaction of at least solving one mystery.

Got you.

He'd known it all along. He would be able to stop this terrible sickness in moments. He just needed to execute the reveal perfectly. He was going to stop Nu from continuing to poison everyone. Wolflock returned to the cabin deck plotting his next move, only to be surprised by the utter stillness. No one was running around, and no one was groaning. There were no sounds or smells of someone being sick. He peeked into the rooms as he went and collected the empty cups, finding the same charred remains in each. The illness may have progressed too far. Maybe they were all too exhausted. He knew who the culprit was. He knew how and why. His mental web had come together just as he'd anticipated.

The only person who didn't look well yet was Mothy. His skin was still clammy, and he was sleeping on his back in a neat bed. As Wolflock collected his cup, he roused for a moment.

"From prince to maid, I see? Oh, how the mighty are humbled..."

Wolflock chuckled and wiped Mothy's thin blonde hair back off his face.

"You'll be well soon, my friend. I'm getting close to the source."

But Mothy was asleep again. He didn't move an inch when Gege let out a terrified squeak from the hall or when one of the cups was smashed on the wall.

"This is not the medicine I said to prepare!" Nan Ji roared and threw another cup, causing it to splash on one of the hallway landscapes. "This will not help these people! I told you to follow my instructions directly!"

"F-father, I did! I didn't change it at all!"

"Then why is this charred!? The recipe doesn't call for charring! I could smell the change!"

"We are trying to rest," Veluse emerged in the hall, wrapped in his blanket. "Keep it down. Also, it tastes better charred. That lovely smoky flavour feels like just what I needed."

"It is not about the flavour! You are not a physician! Feminine men like yourself do not have the strength to work with medicine."

Veluse, who stood at least a foot taller than Nan Ji, glared daggers at the old man.

"Like it's hard to throw a few herbs together and boil them up? Don't make me laugh. If your children are able to perform medicine better than you, I'd say the bar is pretty low."

"What did you say?" Nan Ji growled through gritted teeth.

"Listen, your child brought me the medicine. If anyone's changed it, it's them and they're too frightened to tell you they can do a better job than you. Now be away. My presence requires your absence!"

With a flick of his hair and an extreme incline of his nose, he marched back into his room and shut the door. Wolflock felt a few more of his mental web come together. The culprit had changed the medicine, relying on Nan Ji's bad eyesight and the fact that his children delivered the medicine to keep the changes hidden.

Nan Ji stood outraged and bewildered, his mouth agape. Before he could explode again, Wolflock slipped behind him and up onto the deck. Given the old man's state of shock, he'd only have a few minutes maximum to do what he needed to do.

He burst into the dining hall to find Nü dropping something into the cauldron being used to make everyone's medicine. Her eyes shot to him and she tucked her hands behind her back, her hair coming out of its braid, flying about from the heat of the cauldron.

"Funny how much your hair gets in the way when you're missing this," he held up the glittering hairpin.

Rhiannon D. Elton

CHAPTER 7

Right Under Your Nose

Where did you find that?"

Wolflock smirked, "Oh I think you know where."

"I can explain." She bit her lip, her eyes darting back and forth to the door.

"Oh, I don't think that's necessary. I have all the explanations I need from what I've learned. I've known there was something about you that was different. There was never any question that you were a physician. You have shown glimpses of this to everyone in bits and pieces, but I knew it was more than a passing hobby when your brother and you had verbal slip ups regarding who knew what. He's no expert. You are. A second language is hard to lie in. You're better than your brother in that area, as your face is quite poised, but it's your hands. You're like Mothy. When you're distressed, you clench your skirt. Whenever you feel like you need to hold back, you grip it so tightly your knuckles go white.

"I grew suspicious when Nan Ji began yelling that his formula had been changed and the wrong herbs had been brought up to the kitchen. You were quite specific about the right herbs, whereas your brother, the so-called medical genius, let me do whatever I pleased in the hull. You were relying on his bad eyesight and the fact that he always sent you and your brothers to give the medicine. As long as he stayed distant, he wouldn't see your adaptations.

"But why? Why would you change your father's formula? Was it because you thought you knew better and saw flaws in his diagnosis? That would be evident by your distress last night at dinner. Don't get me wrong; were my father to completely deny my abilities, I'd want to upstage him too."

Nü shook her head, still glancing back to the door. She twitched as if she wanted to grab her hairpin and run, but she was trapped in the kitchen.

"After seeing the herbs you'd practiced charring,

the exchanged mixture in all of these cups and the markers of who you had treated hung above their doors, and you being the last person to enter the kitchen before people started falling ill, I knew it was you. You saw this as an opportunity to finally get the recognition you deserve and, after years of learning and loving your craft, you had it all snatched away. So, you thought that by poisoning the tuiti fruit stew and healing everyone you would be able to be recognised by your father and be able to take up your studies again."

Nü froze, snorted and burst out laughing.

Not the dainty laugh Mothy had drawn from her, but a honking donkey laugh that made her double over, slapping the floor.

Wolflock blinked.

"What... what's so funny?"

She continued to cackle maniacally until she couldn't breathe anymore. Finally, she exhausted herself and locked up to see Wolflock with a look of immense irritation and his arms folded tightly.

"I am so sorry!" she wheezed as she stood up and wiped her eyes. "I have had no sleep. My emotions are... unrestrained." She laughed again, but managed to pull herself together faster. "I still do not know where the poison is coming from, but, I can assure you, Mr

Wolflock, that it is not from me. And, no. I do not want my father to know any of this. He does not have all the information that I have. Once he has settled on a diagnosis, he never changes his mind. My brother and I are far more flexible. The formula I have been giving to the ill people is stopping their bleeding. But you are right. This is not a virus or a transmitted illness. It is a poison."

"What's so funny though?"

"Mothy said you would say this if you found out. He did an impression of you finding everything out and being horrified that I do not want anyone to know I am helping."

"But... why don't you want people to know?" Wolflock frowned, confused.

Nü opened her mouth to answer him but, on queue, Nan Ji stormed in, followed by Gege and Didi. Nü's demeanour changed immediately. She wiped her eyes, bowed her head and stood silently, backing away as her father approached.

"Who," he growled in a low, seething tone, "did this to my formula?"

The children stood silently; trading looks behind his back.

Why isn't she speaking up? This is her moment. She gets to finally get the recognition from her father that she-

"WHO DID THIS TO MY FORMULA?"

Wolflock leaped back in shock as the little man went crimson and shouted so ferociously that spit flew everywhere. Still, the Nan children remained silent, trembling in the wake of their father's rage.

"OUT! OUT, ALL OF YOU! GET OUT!"

Wolflock glared at him, but the others scurried out like frightened mice. Finally, he turned on his heel, rolling his eyes.

What a pitiful tantrum. Fuelled by pure arrogance. Monstrous fellow... Wolflock huffed in his mind. The Nan children stood just outside the door, Gege looking up at Nü, who had maintained her stone-like face.

"He's not well again. You have to-" Gege was pleading as Wolflock came out but stopped at the sight of him.

"Why didn't you say anything?" Wolflock growled. "It was the perfect time to-"

"Stop this." She looked at him with one short sharp motion. "You know nothing, and this is not your business. You will stop. It was a fun game to see how long you would take to figure it out. But now the game is done. Say nothing more."

Wolflock felt as if he'd gotten whiplash. One

moment she was quiet and amiable, the next she was laughing like a goose, and now she was speaking to him as if she had authority over him. It was insulting!

"No! I won't stop! What do you think you know that I don't? Why won't you tell your father you've been helping people?"

Nü's stone cold face didn't budge. "You are smart. I am sure you will figure it out."

She went down below deck, but Wolflock caught Gege by the arm before he could follow her. The nervous brother was clearly the weakest link and Wolflock knew he could pry answers from him.

"Who was ill? Why did she go so cold just now? Why won't she tell your father of her medical expertise?"

Gege glanced back and forth anxiously, shaking in Wolflock's grip.

"I-I-I do not know, sir, Mr Wolflock!" he quivered.

Wolflock raised an eyebrow at the frightened little boy.

"I just want to help make the ship well again and there are too many questions. It's hard to tell what is the right course of action. You understand, aye?"

Gege took a moment, but, with a long sigh, he relaxed. "Thank goodness someone understands it! Like, which formula is right? Which symptoms mean what?

Which preparation methods are best? What colour of snot means they are sick with heat or wind? There is too much!"

Wolflock blinked. Was he still in the right conversation?

"Not what I meant but carry on."

"And then there is quantity! Don't get me started about quantity! Did you know there is a berry that, if you put one more than necessary in, it will stop the tummy from healing and cause diarrhoea!? I do not know how she does it. Or even why she does it!"

Wolflock felt the corners of his mouth twitch into a smile. This was it. Gege was going to tell him everything.

"If she just behaved, father would..." As Gege slowed, Wolflock saw realisation creep over his face. "I cannot say anymore."

"It is alright, Gege. It will help me to help Nü find the source if I know why she won't let your father know she is adept."

Wolflock knew this was a lie. He just couldn't fathom why she would reject recognition and he needed to know why so he could eliminate it. It was unjust to restrain a bright mind in his eyes.

"I guess if it is to help Nü... And you did not tell father before. Girls back home do not normally work. It is seen as being a bad husband if your wife has to work too. Mother was an exception. Women can be healers because, sometimes, women have women problems. Most girls just learn how to play music, sew and do girl stuff like take care of the house. Some girls learn how to write poetry to entertain their families. Because baba is such a loved doctor back home, he can choose who Nü marries. That means he gets to choose the man who would be best for her. But father is very protective of her. He is mad all the time, but he loves us. He would not marry Nü to a man she does not like."

"That's all archaic and... well, frankly horrible. But it doesn't tell me why she won't reveal her potential to be a physician to your father."

"She does not tell him because that would be a disgrace. For her to disobey his order to stop studying medicine, and then publicly say she has surpassed him... No one does that. She pretends to know just enough to be useful when treating girls, but not challenge his power."

"Do you mean to tell me that he is preventing his child from learning because he's frightened she'll get sick because she's a girl, and also because he wants to save his reputation?" Wolflock took a deep breath in an attempt to contain his utter frustration at the circumstances.

"I think he thinks he is protecting her from dying... and he is not aware that he is too strong for a room."

"Too strong for a room?"

Gege made a face, searching for the right words.

"Egotistical is the word." Wolflock offered.

"I do not know what that is, so I think so?"

"But why did she get so cold just before? She was laughing at me moments earlier!"

The small black-haired boy twisted his shirt. "Baba will guard the kitchen like an angry tian lu. She thought she was so close to having everyone better. Now they will get better more slowly, and baba may lose respect."

"Fine, fine, fine." Wolflock waved his hand dismissively, "Did your sister ever say what was the cause of the illness?"

Gege shook his head, "She just said you told her."

"What?"

"That is correct. She said you gave her the answer."

"When did she say this?"

"Uh... maybe two days ago? I am not sure. Can I go sleep now, Mr Wolflock, sir?"

Wolflock looked over the poor boy. His clothes may have been fine, but his face was sagging and gaunt, and he looked like he'd aged fifty years over the last three days.

"Yes, Gege. Get some sleep. You've been a great help."

"Thank you, sir!"

And, with that, he slumped off to the cabins.

I gave her the answer? Wolflock pinched his chin and frowned.

He brought forth the image of his mental spider web, swirling around. The threads were loose at the middle. So many lines had been torn out from his theories. All the nineteen people who were ill had something in common. Something Nü had seen. Something he had missed. The very thought twisted his stomach in frustration.

Lost in thought, he ran his hands over the open barrels of tuiti fruit. No movement. Just still, firm fruit slowly becoming acid pink.

"You're a very loud fruit, you know that?" Wolflock grumbled, his head aching. "You're lucky you're subtle enough when you're fresh. Maybe it's not your fault. Maybe it's Goden's choice of spices."

He picked one up and examined it, still thinking about what Nü had said as he peeled and checked over the fruit. The glistening cloudy flesh speckled with black seeds looked perfectly fine. Not even a bruise. He hadn't had breakfast or lunch, so his stomach scratched at his insides like a hungry puppy. He'd forgotten what the fresh fruit tasted like. As his teeth sank into it, the explosion of citrus and sugar filled his mouth. It was quite refreshing, but after just a few bites he was sick of it again.

"You're too sweet." He sighed and threw it over the edge of the ship, watching several maramuti scatter away from it.

He made his way to the kitchen, seeing Goden preparing to make lunch. He looked bone tired and, when he saw Wolflock approach, his face went red and his eyes glassy.

"Now I don' wanna hear any complaints about me cookin'!" he huffed.

Wolflock shook his head. "Your cooking is adequate, Goden. I just prefer variety in flavours and textures. I also lack what is known as a sweet tooth."

"Yeh borin', is what yeh sayin'," the older man rolled his eyes. "Not like Mothy. He'll eat the ship to the core if we let 'im. I've given 'im four bowls of breakfast and he's still hungry! Well, can' do nuthin' about that. Or the menu. Cap'in's orders til we're outta fresh fruit. Come and 'elp me with a barrel."

"No. I'd rather not." Wolflock shrugged flatly.

Goden rolled his eyes again and slumped to the door.

"Try the one by the mainmast. I checked it earlier and didn't see any river bug larvae." Wolflock called out.

The big man stopped, tensed, then carried on as if he hadn't heard him.

Wolflock sat on the kitchen counter and pinched his chin as he thought. He felt something brush passed his elbow and start rifling through his trouser pocket. A young maramuti had checked and see if he had anything worth swapping for the fruit in its hand.

"Now, now," he smiled. "Kitchen policy is that anyone planning on cooking washes their hands. Since you've not washed yours, I must ask you to be off now."

He picked up the creature like a toddler and popped him out the window, closing it before he could come back in.

"They're always in here," came a stiff voice from behind him. "Swapping things and messing up the kitchen."

Wolflock looked back to see Stra, pale, clammy and slightly buckled in pain.

"You're unwell too, Stra?" Wolflock asked politely.

"Aye... seems to have struck everyone but a few. Have you discovered the culprit?"

"I thought I had it, but alas, my hypothesis came to

no avail. Any thoughts, yet, on the cause?"

"Not a clue."

Wolflock watched him prepare a simple sliced tuiti fruit sandwich and hobble off again. As he left, Goden re-entered with a heavy barrel.

"Check it did yeh, lad? Are yeh blind?" He slammed the barrel down in front of Wolflock, shaking the fruit within.

Frowning, Wolflock hopped off the counter and examined the fruit. Just under the surface layer of motionless fruit squirmed five or six fat larva, grossly squelching to the surface of the barrel.

"That," Wolflock gagged, "is foul. But they were not there when I checked earlier."

"Fish 'em out and chuck 'em over the side," Goden sighed, bringing last night's stew back to the boil.

"Isn't it time to clean out that cauldron? How many days has it been brewing for?"

"Listen 'ere, lad. When you're asked to cook for thirty odd people on no sleep for more days than yeh should, you get to tell me 'ow to cook. Now, get them grubs out and scram!"

Wolflock's stomach twisted harder than before. He hadn't seen anyone clean out the main cauldron for a few days now. He was just grateful there was no meat in it; that would have gone off. He plucked the squishy, rough crustacean larvae out of the barrel, putting them into a bucket, and dumped the fruit onto the bench. There had been only five, which made Wolflock suspicious. Had they just been placed there after he'd left?

He hauled the buckets to the port side of the ship. Just as he was about the empty the bucket over the side of the ship, he heard a tumultuous commotion from the stairs to the cabin deck.

"INSOLENT! STUPID! WRETCHED!"

Wolflock rolled his eyes and sat the bucket down. Nan Ji was shouting again and, when he'd finished with every insult he could muster in common Puinteylien, he continued in Xiayahn. It was when Wolflock saw who he was yelling at that his gut dropped.

Nan Ji was hauling Nü up to the top deck, both of them covered in blood. Wolflock's first thought was that Nan Ji had beaten her so savagely that he'd cut her skin, but, as he darted forward to help, he saw the blood was splattered across the front of her dress.

"HOW DARE YOU!" Nan Ji continued to scream at the top of his lungs. "INSUBORDINATION!"

Wolflock jumped between them and pushed the man away. "Compose yourself, man! This behaviour is barbaric!"

"Stay out of this! Your insolence has corrupted my child! She has been meddling with herbs and consorting with that sick brat! She has brought dishonour to me and this family!"

Nü shook her head, tears streaming down her cheeks as she crawled forward to her father.

"Baba, no! No! Please!"

"You will be silent! If I hear a word from you or see you speaking with anyone, I'll send you to the Hetarai!"

Nü hiccupped a sob, bringing her fist to her lips and crying as Nan Ji stormed off to the kitchen, just as Goden began bringing the first bowls of lunch to the cabins.

"She is not hurt?" Goden asked gently.

Wolflock grasped Nü by the shoulders, checking her over as she tried to push him away.

"I think she's fine. Nü, whose blood is this?"

"Look after 'er, Wolflock." Goden nodded and carried on with his duties.

"Nü. Whose blood is this?" Wolflock breathed, already shaking his head at the answer. Realisation swept over him like a cold chill.

She wept, shaking her head, defeated.

"It is Mothy's."

CHAPTER 8

Healing a Poison Requires a Rope

Wolflock's throat dropped into his gut.

"He was getting better! What happened?"

Nü couldn't speak. She wept into her fists and then opened them forward helplessly, shook her head, and buried her face in her hands again.

She said you gave her the answer. Gege's words echoed in Wolflock's head. He had a flash of memory and saw himself pouring the tuiti fruit plate over the side of the ship. Nü had responded strangely, but he saw now that that was the moment she had figured it out.

"It is the tuiti fruit!" he breathed. "But, how? The

cooks are too thorough with the preparation to let one slip into the food."

"That," she hiccoughed, "is what I have been trying to find these last few days. I did not think it was important to act quickly because everyone was recovering. But Mothy has eaten so much! It completely ruined my medicine. Baba kept telling him to eat. I could not be sure if it was the fruit, so I said nothing. I said nothing!"

Nü gripped her stomach and folded herself down as small as she would go, crying into her knees.

"How do we fix this?" Wolflock asked out loud, gripping his hair and scrunching his face in thought.

"Baba will not let me near him or any of the herbs now. He will keep feeding him and Mothy does not know any better. Unless we find the root cause... I am so scared..."

Wolflock felt her hopelessness and snarled. The cage of sickness that had engulfed the ship had shrank even more until it felt like it was crushing his chest. In an attempt to break out of it he picked up one of the river bug larva and hurled it off the side of the ship as hard as he could. The maramuti who had gathered with their tuiti fruit in had copied him, thinking it was a game. He punched the taffrail and threw another grub. The maramuti began racing around him excitedly, throwing the rest of the larvae into the water. He slumped to the ground, resting his head between the balustrade.

As he heaved a sigh and watched the slimy creatures sink into the depths of the grey water, he felt something spark in his mind. He tried to push it out with his melancholy, but he couldn't help but notice something. The tuiti fruit the maramuti had thrown floated downstream. The river bug larvae sank.

The river bug larvae sank.

His mental web of clues all made sense now.

"Nü! Nü look!"

She sniffed back her tears and joined him at the rails, kneeling down to put her head through them too.

"What is it? I do not see."

"Exactly! The poisonous larva sink!"

She looked at him in confusion, but her eyes began to expand the more the information set in.

"We must hurry!"

She withdrew from the balustrades but Wolflock couldn't move.

"Uh... Nü? I... I think I'm stuck."

Without a sound she put her foot on the taffrail, grabbed his shoulders and pulled with surprising strength. He felt like his head would come off. He landed on his back as he was freed, quickly scrambling to his feet and racing toward the kitchen, Nü close behind.

As they threw open the doors and ran inside, Wolflock saw a maramuti shoot out of the window he had closed before. The cauldron fire was only embers, but it was hot enough that Wolflock and Nü both had to wrap their arms in wet towels before heaving the cast-iron pot onto its side. The contents of the thick stew splashed all over the kitchen and onto the dining hall floor, smothering the embers, rugs and tiles.

Wolflock grabbed a knife and went to work on any of the larger pieces or whole tuiti fruit. He got down amongst the foul gloopy stew of the sickly-sweet fruit and began chopping. None were moving, but he suspected, and after the fifth fruit it was confirmed, that there were dead river bug larvae amongst the fruit. As he sliced it open a dark blue ooze soaked the blade, and he saw the fleshy inside of the giant grub.

"See! I... *Blergh!*" the acrid smell of the decaying creature touched his nostrils and stung, causing him to wretch.

Nü approached him and drove her thumb into his wrist, taking away the nausea nearly instantly.

"Just one of those in an entire cauldron is enough to poison everyone on board. How many are there?" she put her fist to her lips, biting her lip.

Wolflock kept cutting. "Five. There were five. The maramuti must have seen the cooks put tuiti fruit in there and thought that was how to swap things. They're able to eat these creatures, they must have thought we were able to eat them too."

Nü nodded, her brown still furrowed with anxiety. "What do we do now?"

"We tell your father. But first," Wolflock moved to the window and latched it from the inside. "We know the entire course of events. While we were eating lunch on the deck, maramuti must have come in here and put the larva in the pot. Then as the crew members got ill, and the stew was meatless, the cooks just kept adding to the pot, rather than cleaning it regularly. I mean, I can see why. This thing is so heavy!

"Because the larva sink in water, even when cooked the cooks didn't see them in there. That's why every time someone grew ill, it was after they'd eaten the stew. My stomach has been sore ever since I watched Goden cook earlier, and I've only eaten one fresh fruit and the hempseed bread. Your family has served themselves meals you've had prepared from home. Goden and Hognut have been the ones cooking the food, so, of course, they're saturated with it. Like me, they just have gravitated away from it. Canhop, the third mate, only eats raw food, so he didn't eat the stew either. Yifi has been too busy caring for everyone else to eat the cooked food and Fuhji has had morning sickness and was completely put off by the smell of the fruit entirely.

"You've been secretly aiding everyone after you realised it was some kind of poisoning, rather than a contagious illness. I found your attempted blend on Veluse's belongings, but I knew it wasn't his because you'd been using a candle and his paints are flammable. Luckily, you're very careful."

Nü's eyes went wide in horror at Wolflock's last statement. "Charring herbs stops bleeding, so I thought that, if I charred the whole mix, it would stop all the bleeding and people could recover. I knew the tuiti fruit had something to do with it when my family did not fall ill. My brother, Gege, gets sick more than anyone I know. His high stress lowers his wei qi too much. How are we going to help Mothy, though? Baba will not let me go near any of the herbs, and he has told my brothers the same. After he found me with Mothy, he will be guarding him like a tian lu."

"You have to tell me what a tian lu is later, but for now, I have a plan."

The pair of them shared all the information that they could think of. Nü explained the likely process her father would follow, the frequency of medicine giving and the herbs she would need to create an antidote.

"Why does your father's formula make Mothy so ill?"

"I think it is the xing ren herb. It is toxic, but good for coughs and wheezes. It is the main ingredient in the formula father thinks will work."

They both concluded that Nan Ji would be especially watching Mothy's room and the kitchen, but he couldn't watch both at the same time and he still had to sleep.

"Mint makes him sleepy," Nü said.

"We're going to need more than just us in on this." Wolflock thought about who Nan Ji had particularly offended and how to win them over.

It was as easy as asking to get Yifi and the recovered Veluse, Didi and Gege in on the game. They set up a watch between the kitchen, cabins, and Nü's workspace hidden behind the dining hall. Yifi was sent down to the hull to retrieve the herbs Nü needed by hiding them in Wolflock's satchel. She made it passed Nan Ji easily by simply turning up her nose as she walked by with a lady-like "Hmph!".

Nü measured and prepared the formulae. Wolflock, Yifi and Gege rolled the old cauldron out behind the dining hall for her while Nan Ji had a nap, setting up a little fire and pan inside of it so she could char the herbs appropriately. To mask the smell, Gege boiled the mint tea that he would feed to his father in order to make him sleepy. With their current set up they could only make three cups of herbs at a time, which meant Nü had to be preparing them continuously for nine hours to get all the sick their needed doses. When Wolflock broke down the math for her she nodded. Filled with determination, she kissed her hairpin and put her hair up tightly.

Next, Veluse was on distraction duty. Whenever Nan Ji would come to collect more decoction, which he was set to do three times before bed, Veluse had to 'accidentally' knock the tray to spill the mixture, or otherwise delay him. He had to be as annoying as possible, especially between rooms. Gege had to pander to his father and say he would go and get more, but do so as slowly as possibly under the pretense of taking the utmost care. Didi was also able to help with the distraction by playing with the maramuti right in Nan Ji's path.

After collecting all the necessary herbs for Nü, Yifi was to maintain the rope Wolflock tied around his waist as he swung down the outside of the ship and replaced Nan Ji's decoction with Nü's. As he was tying off his rope,

Hognut walked past.

"What in Houl's name are yeh lot doin'?" he grunted, cleaning his pipe.

"Swinging down to the rooms to swap out Nan Ji's potion." Wolflock flashed a completely nonchalant smile to the grouchy crewman as Yifi stared on in astonishment.

"O' course yah are..." Hognut sighed, tapped his pipe and walked away.

Each cabin had a bedside table that sat just under their window. If Nan Ji allowed Gege to distribute the medicine, it was his job to open the porthole windows for Wolflock to get into. If he didn't, it was up to Veluse.

As Wolflock dropped down with Nü's first cup of medicine, trying not to spill a drop, he heard Veluse at Dlumi's window.

"A bit of fresh air will do you the world of good, m'darling."

Wolflock swung back and forth carefully until he hooked his leg on the round frame. In an awkward but precise motion, he swapped the cups and tipped Nan Ji's medicine into the water. He did that for both sides of the ship and the Captain's room. He had believed that he would get ample downtime between drops, but at the rate he could deliver the medicine and the speed Nü produced it, as well as corresponding with Nan Ji's prescribed times, he had to refashion the rope into a seated harness instead of a belt.

Hour by hour, the sun dropped and the faces of the ill grew brighter. Wolflock was particularly careful of Mothy, though. His friend was barely conscious, and his fever hadn't subsided. When he coughed, blood still came up, but not nearly as much as Nü was still splattered with.

When Goden came to the kitchen to make dinner, Wolflock tried to lean casually on the taffrail with Yifi, his breath bated.

"Hognut! Hognut!" Goden shouted. "The bloody maramuti nicked me pot!"

The both of them glanced up at the great bearded man, pipe in beard and sails being pulled up for the night as the anchor was dropped.

Would he give them away? Had he seen the potion making set up behind the dining hall?

He chewed on his pipe and eyed Goden for a long moment.

"Bloody mongrels."

"I know right!? And they spilt the soup everywhere! What are we gonna have for tea?"

Hognut chewed a bit more.

"Sammiches."

"Sammiches?"

"Sammiches."

"Sammiches." Goden agreed thoughtfully.

Wolflock and Yifi breathed a sigh of relief, and she dropped him over the ledge for the last time of the evening. He deposited the last cup to Parihaan and climbed back up. The six of them celebrated a job well done with Goden's delicious garlic butter 'sammiches' and some hot tea. Nü felt guilty about the mess they'd left for Goden and offered their assistance to clean the floor. Wolflock tried to slip away but Hognut and his beard blocked the door.

The kitchen was finally free of tuiti fruit and it smelled wholesome and pure again, with a strong hint of clove oil. As they played cards in the fresh kitchen, a few of the other passengers came up for a breath of fresh air, but no Mothy. He was thankful to see Slavidus and Captain Blutro return, and even more so, when they hoisted the anchor and sent Goden and Hognut straight to bed.

"I just wanted to thank you again, Nan Ji, for all your hard work. On behalf of the ship we cannot express our gratitude," Captain Blutro shook his hand graciously.

"A doctor's work is never done," Nan Ji smiled saccharinely.

"I suppose not. I heard Mothy coughing and wheezing earlier. I hope he hasn't recovered just to get something new."

"I'll check on him in the morning. He has had enough medicine tonight. It must be given time."

The night drew on in a quiet celebration and more passengers joined them for a short time before returning to bed. Tired, sore and satisfied with the execution of their plan, Wolflock bid his partners in crime goodnight and retired for the evening as well. Mothy's face was still alarmingly hot, but his arm and leg had started to fall out of the bed, which Wolflock took as a good sign.

That evening he dreamed he could smell Nü's potion still, and that someone paced up and down the hall, but he couldn't see who. When he was jostled away by a maramuti licking his ear, his dreams made sense. His door had slid open a fraction and he could see a bundle of fabric on the ground. He put on his deep red monogrammed slippers and dressing gown. The bundle of fabric was Nü, leaning against the wall with her legs tucked in.

"Nü? Why are you outside my room?"

Her dark eyes, heavy with black bags sagging under them, moved slowly over him. Her chest sank with her breath and she hummed to try to warm up her words.

"I am not outside your room. I... I am. But I am really outside Mothy's room."

"Is he better?"

She smiled. "His fever has broken. I can hear him snoring."

Wolflock grinned and peeked into the room, seeing his friend in one of his normal sleeping positions with his legs tangled around his pillow and his face drooling on the floor.

"We did it."

They both smiled at each other and Wolflock saw that same sparkle in Nü's eyes that he saw in Mothy's. Defiant, kind, determined, but good. The sparkle muted as she looked towards the stairs.

Nan Ji's ramie cloth trousers appeared as he brought down a decoction. It had a stronger odour than the ones he'd made yesterday, but Wolflock stepped back as he approached. Nü struggled to her feet, looking at her father in horror.

He moved towards Mothy's room.

Rhiannon D. Elton

CHAPTER 9

Smiles, Secrets & Sacrifices

"Why are you here, Nü?" Nan Ji frowned, putting his hand on Mothy's door.

Nü said nothing but jumped forward and blocked the path.

"What are you doing? This is for him."

"Baba I cannot..." she said breathlessly, "I cannot let you do this."

"What are you talking about? Stand aside."

"N-No!"

"Move or I will make you."

"No!" she raised her voice and slapped the cup,

151

sending it clattering to the wall and spilling the contents across the room. "I will not let you!"

Nan Ji stepped back, astounded that his daughter stood eye to eye with him.

"What is the meaning of this?" he growled. "I am trying to save this boy's life and you-"

"You aren't saving him." Wolflock spat angrily and stood by Nü. "You're using him as verification that you aren't a failed, inflexible, unlearning practitioner. You're sacrificing him to satisfy your own pride because you can't stand the idea that one of your children knows more than you. The formula you made never worked! It made everyone worse! And so, your child changed it in secret to save your face!"

"Lies!" Nan Ji hissed. "You are an insolent liar!"

"Then why was Mothy still dying!?"

"Where is your proof!?"

"It is true, baba," Nü whispered, shaking nervously as Gege emerged with dark eyes as well, clearly having slept as much as Nü.

Wolflock grinned.

He had coughed and wheezed deliberately from Mothy's room through the day and evening, making sure that the Captain and Nan Ji heard. Nü had said the key herb that would hurt Mothy was one that was used for coughing and wheezing, so he had devised a plan to get Nan Ji to bring Mothy extra medicine. While she was in this exhausted state, her emotions would be less restrained and she would finally admit to her father that she was just as skilled as he was, if not more.

"Gege saw that it was a poison in the tuiti fruit stew that was the cause."

Nan Ji and Wolflock blinked.

"What?"

"He did not want to dishonour you, so he did not correct you, but Gege believed that he knew of a more effective formula, so he changed it. I have been helping him with the decoction, as there were a lot of herbs and measurements for such a complex formula and he needed more hands. That is why you saw me delivering his medicine yesterday."

All three of them looked shocked at her words. Wolflock was in shocked disbelief that she wasn't coming clean. He had lined this up perfectly and, like a koi fish, she had evaded his trap. Her father ignoring her intelligence was a crime in his eyes.

There was a very long, awkward silence that grew like a thick plant between them all. Nan Ji turned to Gege, staring at him with unblinking, critical eyes.

"Is this true?"

The frail boy swallowed. "Y-yes, baba?"

"What is wrong with my formula?"

Wolflock noted a very slight change in his tone, as if he was conceding defeat to a foe mightier than he.

"You... umm... the patients were suffering from... umm... poisoning... umm... from the umm... Tuiti fruit. It was not.... umm... a pathogen..." he winced as if he'd received a blow, but Nan Ji pulled his thin beard thoughtfully.

Wolflock looked at Nü, waiting for her to speak, but she kept her head bowed, moving her lips as if she was still giving Gege instructions on what to say. She'd clearly told her little brother everything he needed to know to convince their father that he was the one who had changed the formula, and that would be enough to keep Nan Ji's views affirmed.

Wolflock saw right away that Nü had been two steps ahead of him this whole time. She had guarded Mothy's room, thinking Nan Ji may try to give him one more dose of medicine, and she had rehearsed their lines with Gege to make the story believable enough to fool their father.

"Show me what you did," Nan Ji asked with less suspicion.

"Umm... well... I..."

"He used a cleansing and blood correcting formula from Dong Wai Din's scroll. Number fifty-six," Nü said quickly and took her brother's hand in support. "I remember seeing it."

Nan Ji seemed satisfied with their response, for he smiled and nodded. "You may have saved young Mothy's life, my clever boy. Let me make you some tea."

Gege nodded, not letting go of Nü's hand, and they headed to the kitchen. Wolflock growled and clenched his fists, glaring at Nan Ji he turned on his heel and stalked away. He knew he should have been pleased with the result. Nan Ji was no longer poisoning Mothy, and he would recover, but he hated that Nü had to lie about her skills. It just didn't feel fair. Why should she diminish her talent for the sake of someone else's pride?

After stomping to his room, then out again, back into it and out again, so frustrated he didn't know where he actually wanted to go, he settled on checking on Mothy. Someone had cleaned him up and changed his clothes. Even his hair had been washed. Wolflock, in his current mood, felt as if Nü had greatly invaded Mothy's privacy if she had been the one to do it, which he suspected she was.

After pacing three steps back and forth in Mothy's cabin, he huffed and sat on the chair at the desk, rapping his long fingers.

"You'd probably be confused at why I'm so upset," he spoke to Mothy's snoring form. "I just don't understand it! I know you'd tell me that everyone is different, and they have their own path in life to tread. You'd probably say that you understand why I'm upset and then you'd talk about how not everyone needs recognition to feel good about themselves. Then you'd say sometimes it's just the act of helping people that brings fulfilment. To that I say, no wonder you like her if you see that in her. I for one, do not and shall not."

He paused, frowning as Mothy's snores grew quieter.

"There are so many things about the last few day's events that do not sit right with me, though. My normal intuition has been thwarted and I don't know why. Firstly, I'm certain you felt ill before the food fight and the picnic lunch, during which I suspected the maramuti contaminated the stew. Also, where did the handkerchief I found come from? My gut says it is suspicious and I don't know where to look for the answers. Something is not right and, although my mind tells me that this case is solved, my gut says otherwise."

Mothy gave a loud snore in response.

"You're right... I shall be grateful the ship is

moving at top speed again and that you are well. Perhaps things will be revealed in the future. This was an illuminating discussion. I'll let you rest."

As he departed, he heard music strike up on the top deck and some mid-morning singing blossom into the air. Smiling, he ascended into the warm sunlight, leaning on the railing to watch the renewed festivities. The children were playing with the maramuti and skipping to the tune played on Groger's accordion.

As he enjoyed the warm sun parting through the light clouds, Wolflock felt a tickle at his elbow. A maramuti was grooming his arm hair. The creature gave his skin a sniff and then... SMACK.

It whacked his arm hard with a long flat dried piece of bark.

"Ouch!"

The critter dove into the water, leaving him the crispy item.

"Thanks a lot..." he huffed.

Wolflock picked up the strange bark and looked at it more closely. The distinct veins and frill made him stop. It was a dried river bug larva. But it wasn't the same colour as the bright pink and green ones he was used to. This was a deeper purple and blue. Did it turn that way when it was dried?

"*Shi no namekuji*," came a soft voice from his right.

His sharp blue eyes fell upon Nü. She was gripping his skirt gently but was smiling.

"I don't speak Xiayahn."

"That's an ingredient for assassins. The sea slug of death. We use Hai Shen in tonics. They're also sea slugs. You can only get them in the ocean. I wonder where it found it here. I do not think it is in our stores."

Wolflock said nothing. He didn't want to converse with her at all. Even if she had just laid another mystery at his feet.

"I am not sorry for evading your trap, Wolflock. I am very thankful you helped me give medicine to the ship."

"Yes, well. One day, you'll have to let your father know about your talents. Mothy gave me a good perspective on the situation."

Nü's smile filled her eyes as she looked coyly away. "He is good for that. I am glad he is better."

A familiar maramuti climbed up her shirt and leaped across to Wolflock, grooming his hair as he pat its leg.

"Oh, hello there."

"You make strange friends," Nü giggled.

"This one, I believe, has been quite warm in my room for the past few nights. They are very entertaining creatures. Much like people."

The maramuti drew a louse from his hair and munched on it gleefully.

"Ah... ew. You can have that."

The maramuti reached into a hidden pouch on its stomach and pulled out a particularly thick sea bug that was still wriggling. Wolflock jumped back as it smacked the slug on the railing four times quickly, killing it and then placing it on Wolflock's hand.

"Umm... really... there's no need. I didn't want the louse anyway," he tried to explain, revolted by the slimy, squishy dead slug on his hand.

The maramuti looked at him with its big round eyes expectantly, from the slug to Wolflock, clearly not seeing his discomfort.

"Uh..." he groaned in confusion, but finally accepted the slug by pinching it with his index finger and thumb. "Thanks?" he offered tentatively and put the slug in his trouser pocket, feeling it squish wetly.

Satisfied, the maramuti scurried along the railing to join the others. As soon as it was out of sight, he took the slug from his pocket and examined it, ready to throw it overboard.

"After they are dried it can be used for stomach aches if used in very small doses. Or they can become a lethal poison."

She wants the slug. Wolflock thought irritably, wanting to throw it overboard to spite her.

"From what I've seen they're pretty lethal fresh."

"They can kill a grown man in a day if eaten dried. The poison becomes concentrated. That is all I meant." She paused for a moment, rubbing her arm. "Pennyroyal and tansy help keep lice away. Lots of things do. I could make you and Mothy some hair wash if you like. For the lice."

Wolflock thought for a moment. She was apologising without apologising. She was conducting a truce.

"I would like that. But first, tell me why you won't let others know you are adept at medicine? I'm afraid we cannot be friends unless I know."

Nü sighed. "Before mama was killed by sickness, baba was so happy to have such a talented and clever daughter. He encouraged me and smiled a lot. After she died, he was scared he would lose me, too. He was told that women are not as strong as men and that I needed to be kept safe. He is angry because he knows I love medicine and he desperately wants to teach me, but he cannot. He hates that my brothers show no promise, so he lies to himself. I love healing. I love it with every inch of my being. I will never stop, but I cannot hurt my father. He is so sad.

"Were I to publicly go against his wishes, it would dishonour him. I would ruin our family name. People would doubt his ability to heal. You may be surprised, but he is a very good doctor. He just does not learn easily, and there are so many different diseases in other countries. By pretending to the world that I am obeying his wishes, our family is held in high regard. This means my brothers will be able to choose to marry women of good position and wealth, and I can stay under baba's roof until I want to marry."

"So, by being trapped in one way, you're free in a more important way."

Nü nodded with a knowing smile. "Are we not all?"

Wolflock didn't really know what to say to that, so he held his tongue.

"Shall we go and get Mothy some lunch?" he finally offered, hoping his friend was now awake.

"As long as it is not tuiti fruit!"

They both chuckled, nearly bumping into Grogen as he carried out the breadbasket.

"Oh, thank you, Grogen. We were just coming to-
"

Grogen knocked Wolflock's hand away and tutted.

"Nah, lad. The bread's no good. Shoulda been thrown out days ago."

Wolflock's eyes went wide. "What do you mean?" It was all he'd eaten for four days.

"Nah. It's gone off. Moldy. Fresh tuiti fruit is all ya'll get til tomorrow."

Wolflock's gut flipped and felt his face going green.

 "What do you mean it's mouldy!?"

The Case of the Curse of Houl

Dire Mama,   Guimpus der 18ⁿ ʃʃn
Gulao Rosara

        J bin ʒʒmnig bittted ʃʃn mich neuen bekannt an
der Schpp.
        Ji Glauben J werde nicht macht daʒu freunde und
oan J betege ʃi wiret oinet mehr.
        J hab oinet gemacht oin oahr Gut freund ʃʃm
Mythy, ʃʃ ʃʃoharig oxoahnt oin mich noulig lahtere. Je
ʃi kannen otollar der Schpp ij oin ʃʃn ʃʃber platʒoxo ao
oxaʃ kannen pax ʃʃ haben uf ʃi oxaffen ʃʃ. ʒa oxx hab.
Wir hab oxfandent ʃib Gothe und uxoocht mehr alo unoxam
meʃʃm toilen ʃʃn lachnet und fxohlichxit. Wir protehat
ʃuxch oin oxlxt ʃʃn ʒonu magxlxxnet Gaʃ und hab oinet
nux onfallant ʒa oxoxuch maxomut! Gah oinʃ maʃich
Gohhphe und hab Gegeben uno ʒuno ʃʃn untoxhautlen unʃ
untoxouch.
        Gxxch ʃʃngo oxGotuno oin neuen Klappe Schwimme
Gah ʒu der Schpp uno Klottoxn ambxxʃ.
        Gah oinʃ ʃʃ oxxochxdon ʃʃ der Loute an der Schpp. J
oxll oxxouch uno ʃʃʒʒxhx ʃi oin.
        Gxch ij fathox? Jʒ Oxennan Gut? J auch auofahx
micht hottoxhat oin ʒukunft lahtoxo abox kumʃ jotʒt J muʃ
ʃʃ of. Unhna ij untoxxich uno abox tuxx oxxt.

Dire Mama,   Gxxlamuo der 18ⁿ ʃʃn
Gulao Rosara

        Mythy hat abgxfallig oxunk. J kannxcht Schlafen. J…
J bin botxoffen. J bin nicht ʒo botxoffen ʃat J oxde klxk
Gah alle nacht. abox J muʃ ʒugeben ʃat ʃʃ oxde ʃʃ
botoxtxigonot ʒu hox thxm Gohnligh Schxoxht ʃuxch ʃox
maunʃ. Jʃxao iʒ falʃch.
        Bxxxxlight Schlafen oxde aufloxen micht ʒuoxxtʒigh.

Liebe MAMA,   Kampus der 20te sen
Erste Nacht

Endlich iz trunk. I bin soused out. I so nicht
glaube I werde absofal trunk. I bin recht dat hier iz
nicht fur einen trunkhet aber hab nur uroocht absocht.

So iz ein finster thhx, aber nicht es soonicht es
ein sen der Schaffcarbater soonint mir eins Banonnoht.
I werde geben so mehr ausfuhre es I kannen.

Liebe MAMA,   Kampus der 22st sen
Erste Nacht

So sos der maximut soonint ost soonich handelet sen
uns. So fans soonschaft merde einzu der obot haronkopf
unoox suppe soo ein. I loote so alle unht ein hofen uns
endlich iz an der boben. I werde oboomitteln so ein soo
erzahlen gohnt mir oroochen uns. Zurof jetzt. I hab ein
neuen freuns zu obfragen.

Ein soochofinger bruther.

Wolfley J. Felen

About the Author

Rhiannon is the walker between worlds. One foot in Earth, the other constantly stepping into Pelaia. As if gazing into a crystal ball, she sees this other world and all that happens within it with the clarity of someone staring through a veil. It is her purpose in life to transcribe these histories, adventures and mysteries for you to enjoy.

This witchy woman was raised by a fairy who taught her that there are all kinds of magic throughout the world. She taught Rhiannon to withhold judgement because you never truly know another's story. She also taught her that everyone, no matter how flawed, has something to give.

The adventures of Rhiannon's youth lead her through trials and dangers that taught her about the darkness within the world, but it also showed her that anything could be overcome. There was always a way. Surrounded by so much apathy and hopelessness, Rhiannon made it her goal in life to show others the light and that if they could dream it they could do it.

The way she was shown this was through stories.

Stories of friendship, love, adventure, discovery, compassion, understanding, and kindness. All of these stories gave her new friends, new lessons, new life.

In the depths of her darkest place during year 11 and 12, when she felt at her loneliest, drugs surrounded her life in terrible ways, the self worth of those she loved and admired crumbled, she was relentlessly bullied and felt friendless in her most trying years, she lived in squalor due to bureaucratic errors, and yet she still had to be "perfect". She had to perfectly excel in school, she had to perfectly remain calm and gentle in the face of abusive men, she had to be a perfect role model for all those around her. That craving for perfection in order to get love nearly killed her several times. In all of this darkness with politicians sacrificing real people and real environments for imaginary money, with teachers displaying no compassion for their students, with men abusing women and children, with communities vilifying those who needed them most, with injustice reigning and all hope seemingly lost... Puinteyle was born.

All of these pains in life were fixed in Puinteyle.

All of them were able to be mended and healed because of a conscientious effort. The people of Puinteyle wanted to be better than their problems. Puinteyle was where people made an effort to love freely and always sought to help each other, animals and the environment. Harmony. True and beautiful harmony. Where the pendulum never swayed too far away from that beautiful harmonious and happy point of balance.

But like in our lives, there is always obstacles to overcome and darkness to understand. Therefore, Puinteyle would always have its own inner turmoils to learn and grow from too. Thus, the stories never truly end.

Rhiannon has always lived and breathed stories, knowing her role in life is to be this guide through a new world for others. Her dream is to support her community with her stories, as well as creating a company where other artists can come together in celebration of Pelaia and all it has to offer.

Get More of the Magic & Mystery...

subscribe.rhiannoneltonauthor.com/more

If you want more clues, more magic and more mystery, let me know by going to the Case of the Curse of Houl subscribe page.

You'll get clues, maps, sketches, behind the scenes stories, lore and much more! You'll also be the first to know when a new story is coming out so you can solve the mystery before your friends.

If you sign up with the magical link below, you'll also get a free downloadable map to follow Wolflock's journey to Mystentine University.

subscribe.rhiannoneltonauthor.com/more

Thank you for being part of the magic and supporting an independently published Australian author! Australia's independent authors need the support of their local community to continue to produce the books we all love.

If you enjoyed this book, please leave a positive review online (where you purchased the book or on Goodreads), recommend this book to your friends or family, or purchase another copy to gift to a loved one.

Stay tuned for the next mystery in the series:

THE WOLFLOCK CASES

BOOK 4

THE CASE OF THE BITTER DRAUGHT

www.rhiannoneltonauthor.com

  RhiDElton

 RhiannonEltonAuthor

 RhiDElton

 rhiannoneltonauthor

 Rhiannon D. Elton

RhiDElton

THE WOLFLOCK CASES